WE JUST DOWN FOR EACH OTHER

A LOVE STORY

BY: KEILA

© Copyright September 2015 Keila

All rights reserved. No part of this publication may be reproduced, distributed, or transmitted in any form or by any means, including photocopying, recording, or other electronic or mechanical methods, without the prior written permission of the publisher, except in the case of brief quotations embodied in critical reviews and certain other noncommercial uses permitted by copyright law.

This is a work of fiction. Names, characters, places and events are strictly the product of the author or used fictitiously. Any similarities between actual persons, living or dead, events, setting or locations are entirely coincidental.

Jasmine

"Well, Congratulations Ms. Knight, you are eleven weeks pregnant." Doctor Sanders said as she took off her glasses, standing against the sink with paper in her hands that I assumed was my paperwork.

"Are you sure?" I asked surprisingly. Looking at the paperwork she handed me and yes it was true, I was eleven weeks.

"Is this not exciting news?" She asked, noticing the confused look written all over my face.

"Yes, it's very exciting. I'm just shocked that's all." I smiled. The thought of having someone running around the house calling you "Mommy" was a gift from God. I couldn't wait to get home to tell Kenny about the news I'd just received, I just hoped he wouldn't want me to get rid of it.

"Okay Hun. Follow up with me within the next two weeks, and here is your prescription for your prenatal vitamins. You take care of yourself and if you need anything please let us know. We are always here to help." She said as she walked out the door.

I had no clue that I was pregnant. Not once did I crave anything or spit up. Now that I knew, I was going to make sure I ate right, exercised right and didn't let anything or anybody stress me out. Having a baby was something I've always wanted but I guess back then wasn't the perfect timing and God knew exactly what he was doing.

As I gathered my things, I quickly walked out the room making my way to the checkout window. As soon as she handed me my reminder card for my appointment that was scheduled two weeks from today I placed it inside my purse. Part of me wanted to tell Kenny about the pregnancy now but I decided to wait until I got home to tell him. As I thought about calling Lia, I decided to wait and surprise her too, and I knew she was going to spoil my baby no matter what the gender was.

Making it outside the doctor's office, I climbed into my car and drove off. I clicked on the app for my GPS to search for the nearest Walgreens there was and once the information came up, Siri confirmed that it was one up the street, so I headed straight there to get my prescription filled.

Pulling into the parking lot of Walgreens I got out the car and hurried inside so I wouldn't be late for work. Walking into the back heading towards the pharmacy I didn't see anyone waiting so I knew it wouldn't take me a long time.

"Aww, you're expecting? Congratulations." Said the worker.

"Yes, thank you very much." I said giving her all of my insurance information. Once she was finished I turned around, getting ready to leave.

"I'm so sorry." I said as I bumped into someone. I didn't see the face of them but I knew it was a dark-skinned female with some ugly ass blonde hair in her head that needed to come down. Ugh! I hated when people chose to wear a certain hair color that didn't correspond with their skin tone, but it was what they chose, not me.

Making it outside I noticed it'd gotten dark very fast and I couldn't wait to get home. Soon as I pulled out the parking lot I jumped on the highway, doing 80 all the way to my house looking around to make sure their wasn't a police sitting by somewhere.

POP!

It felt as if my tire had just popped off my car. Once I got my car to a complete stop, I hopped out and noticed the tire was flat and I instantly got aggravated. I got back inside, and turned on the caution lights. Reaching over to the passenger seat I grabbed my cell phone from my purse to give Kenny a call, but instead of him answering the lady on his voicemail greeted me. "Great, fucking night." I said to myself.

WHAM! WHAM!

A few minutes later I felt my door being opened and out of nowhere I was hit with two punches to my stomach that caused me fall over in pain. I screamed out loud as my assailant snatched me out of my car. Once I got a peek at my attacker I realized it was the same customer who I had bumped into back at Walgreens. All this over a damn bump? I thought to myself. I wanted to fight back but I couldn't because of all the pain that my stomach was causing me.

"You just ain't gone leave my nigga alone, are you? All the cheating he doing and your dumb ass still around. Get the picture bitch, he don't want you." She yelled as she stretched out her leg and kicked me into the passenger seat with so much force.

"Stop please, you're hurting me." I cried hoping and praying she would leave me alone. I was never the scary type but I had no fight left in me and I damn sure couldn't move. I prayed that everything would soon come to an end and my baby would be okay.

"Get off of her, right now." I heard a deep voice yell. "Are you okay?" The man asked me.

He grabbed me and my belongings and helped me into his car. I was happy that the hospital was close by thanking God that he sent this man to save my life.

***

"Baby, wake up. It's us." Kenny said rubbing my forehead.

Once my eyesight got clear, I looked up to see Kenny and Lia standing over me with tears in their eyes. I tried removing my hands from my side but my body was weak as shit. Once I finally got my hands on my stomach, I asked God to please let there be a baby inside. Deep down inside something told me from the kick she gave me there wasn't a baby anymore. I could feel it.

"Baby, it's gone. We had a miscarriage." He said as he rubbed my stomach.

"It's all your fucking fault. You and your side bitches." I yelled as the tears ran down my face. "Just leave me alone, please." I cried to him. To hear him say miscarriage broke my heart. I was devastated, and felt betrayed not only because of my pregnancy but due to the fact that he kept cheating on me.

"What you talking about?" he asked, acting like he knew nothing at all.

"Get the fuck out. I lost my baby because you couldn't keep your dirty ass dick in your pants. I HATE YOU." I yelled pointing towards the door. He looked at me with sorrow in his eyes but I ignored his look by closing my eyes. Lia came over to my bed side and placed her head against my chest, allowing me to soak up her shirt with the Constant tears falling from my eyes.

"I swear, when we catch this bitch. I'm splitting her pussy open. Fucking up her insides, making sure she won't be able to have kids." She yelled yanking from me, punching holes in the walls.

"Jasmine, get up boo, it's just a dream."

"Huh? Are you sure?" I asked looking around the front lobby.

"Yes, you were kicking and screaming like somebody was attacking you."

Since the day of my miscarriage I'd been dreaming about this for years and it never went away. Some nights I would wake up in cold sweats and the only thing I could do was hold my stomach and cry. Kenny was still lying about everything, so I never talked about it around him. As a woman this was something I will never forget about, something nobody will ever understand. I get that miscarriages are common, but to lose your child from being attacked by one of your niggas side chicks hurt likes hell, who does things like that?

I had to pull myself together because I was at work and I didn't want anyone thinking I was some crazy lady. I'm just happy one of the workers were here to wake me up because ain't no telling what else could have happened. I got up from my cubical and headed towards the bathroom.

Once I made it into the restroom, I walked over to the sink to throw a handful of water on my face, hoping it would remove the sweatiness that caused my forehead and cheeks to shine bright like a damn diamond. Looking in the mirror, I smiled because I was a woman who never gave up or let anything or anyone bring them down. Yes, I had my setbacks, but God made sure I had my major comebacks as well.

***

Instead of me working my regular shift, tonight I ended up doing a double, my body was tired and my eyes felt heavy. Like I needed a cup of coffee or something and I didn't even drink that shit. I couldn't wait to go home to be under my man. The thought of him always made me feel some type of way, you know that love feeling that settled in the bottom of your stomach that I'm sure all women get at some point in their lives over a nigga. So I figured I'll shoot him a call to see what he was up to. Looking at the time on my phone, I had exactly thirty minutes left before I got off and that brought so much joy to my feet because they were hurting like hell. I was working at Holland Home as a Resident Assistant.

I liked my job but it wasn't something I was too comfortable with. This was something I picked up when I moved in with my dude Kenny. I only did it because I wasn't the kind of woman to just sit around waiting on a nigga to give me anything so of course I went out and got it on my own. What type of nigga didn't want his chick to get money anyway?

Not trying to discredit my man or nothing because he wined and dined me and made sure I had and needed everything a woman could ask for, however, I still chose to work some hours to prove to him that his money wasn't all that mattered to me. Money or material things would never be any reason why I dealt with a nigga. I had money saved up in my bank account, my credit score was 720 and with this job, I just continued to stack my money.

I let the phone ring multiple times but he wasn't answering which made me wonder. More than likely he was either sleep or in the streets making money. Knowing him, he's probably mad because I chose to work this double tonight. He didn't approve of the fact that I chose to work, he was the type to take care of his woman but I was the type to handle my own.

He always told me how he wanted his woman to be a housewife: cooking, cleaning, taking care of the children and making sure the bills were taken care of, the typical shit wives did at home. I was cool with that, but being the type of chick I was I couldn't just stay in the house it was a need that I got up and got off my ass. I will never allow a nigga to say "If it wasn't for me".

As a twenty-two year old high school graduate you would think I'd be working my dream job which was a famous fashion designer. I always had a thing for fashion, but that shit changed once Kenny and I decided to get serious. I only attended college for one semester due to the fact I up and moved out of town with Kenny to help him take care of his sick mother, but I was the one who mainly did everything for her. Kenny was too busy running the streets, coming in and out late nights and sometimes he would leave us at home alone. Once my parents found out I quit school to run after a nigga they cut ties with me. I tried reaching out to them a couple of times but they ended up changing their number.

The thought of my parents made my eyes water but I kept it together because I was around a lot of people. About three to four months after I moved out with Kenny and his mom, I got a call from one of my aunties telling me my parents were in a bad accident. Once Kenny and I hopped on the highway, I was receiving another call saying God had just taken my parents away from me and I lost it.

After their death I was weak, heart-broken and sick to the stomach. I didn't understand why God called them home so soon because without them I was nothing and didn't have nobody. I mean my best-friend Lia and Kenny were there for me, but it's nothing like having your own parents by your side. They did everything for me and made sure I was taken care of.

My dad was a lawyer and my mom was a nurse, we weren't the richest but we weren't broke either. They made sure I had everything that I wanted and needed no matter the circumstances. Being the only child was good but boring at the same time because I had nobody to play with growing up.

I rarely went around my family because both sides treated us different and always thought we felt as if we were better than them and that wasn't true. Most of my aunts and uncles were either hoes or crack heads and my parents didn't do the things they did so we had to love them from a distance. Every time we would come around my younger cousins would steal my clothes, shoes, jewelry and electronics just to take it back to their mom and dad to get money for drugs. That's a damn shame to have your kids doing your dirty work when you could get out and get a job.

You would think by us both losing our parent's it would make us closer, but it did nothing but pull us apart because we had mixed emotions that we never shared with one another, and that's what drove the both of us crazy due to us holding so much inside.

Kenny and I didn't have a perfect relationship and neither did anyone else, and that was something I wanted my parents to understand but they always said "love wasn't supposed to hurt". We had good times and bad times but somehow and someway we worked through everything and here we are four years later.

Being together for so long we'd been through hell and back with each other. Bitches, insecurity, and jealousy was the down fall of our relationship and why we had broken up so much. Every relationship has problems and in my eyes nobody was perfect, and mistakes were made.

Kenny and I met back when I had just graduated from high school. Me and Lia was out at the club celebrating, having entirely too much fun, plus this was my first time going out so she made sure I enjoyed myself. Being that we were underage, a girl Lia knew got us some fake ID's and that's how we got in. I'm sure every young chick then had to go through this at some point in their younger life, when we knew our young asses should have just waited until our time came, maybe I wouldn't have never been in this fucked up situation with Kennys' ass.

It was a night of celebration and the club was jumping, every corner throughout the entire club was packed with niggas and bitches. I was kind of nervous because I'd never been out to a club like this. Only fun I ever experienced was block parties and basement parties and those were the shit so I know the club life was going to be worth it, I was due for something new.

I was dressed in my all-white body fitted dress with my Prada pumps to match that I'd been dying to wear.

"It's jumping in here bitch." Said Lia. She was already bouncing her ass around; this wasn't her first time being inside a club so she was already ready to get loose.

Once I got over my fears, we made our way to the dance floor. I was shaking in my panties at first but the drink Lia gave me before we came had finally settled in my system.

Me and Lia was known for dancing and once the DJ started to play Ayy Ladies by Travis Porter it was only right that we fuck the dance floor up.

As we started popping and shaking our ass to the song I felt someone walk up behind me. When I turned and noticed it was a sexy light skin nigga I didn't even have an attitude anymore. Those sexy light skins always did something to a sistah. With his hands gripping my ass I gave him what he wanted, the best dance of his life.

"I see you know what you doing ma." He said grabbing my hips following my every move. He wasn't a dirty nigga I could tell; only thing that threw me off was the foul smell coming from his mouth. I wasn't an alcoholic or a smoker, but I could sense he had been drinking and smoking entirely too much.

"Yeah, I wouldn't be here if I didn't." I responded twerking my ass on his stick. Once I felt his pole rub across my ass I knew it was time for me to stop showing out. I was a virgin and I didn't want to geek this nigga head up having him thinking I was bout that life when I wasn't.

"Why you stop?" He asked me. The look he had on his face was funny as hell to me, expressing that he was enraged by my decision.

"I'm nothing like these other chicks in here, I don't want to have you under the impression that I was coming home with you." I snapped pointing down to his dick. He stepped back, crossed his arms and then laughed. I felt embarrassed, but hey I was just being honest.

"It's nothing like that ma, it's just a dance shorty. But anytime he get attention he tends to get out of hand." He chuckled. "What's your name ma?"

"Ahh the name is Jasmine." I slurred. He had me mesmerized by that sexy ass voice, plus I was a little tipsy.

"My name is Kenny, the one and only." He flirted licking his lips. "Follow me."

Like a dumb ass I followed him to the bar. We talked about so much and I told him my reason of being there. Once he heard me mention I had just graduated he said he was going to get me fucked up and that's exactly what he did. Our conversation was so good I forgot all about Lias' ass, but I knew she was good.

"Girl, snap out of it." said Kema, One of the other workers here. She was cool and could also be a little messy. Every time she came around me I did nothing but stare because something about her appearance was so familiar to me but I couldn't think of any place I could know her from.

"I'm just zoned out chick." I said back. I walked back to my cubical to check my phone to see if I missed a call or something but once again there was nothing from Kenny. I was more worried than anything because he always checked to see if I needed something while I was working and this particular time he didn't. "I hope everything is alright with him." I mumbled to myself.

After checking my phone my mind drifted back to me and Kennys' past, after we started to hang out and spending every day with each other we became girlfriend and boyfriend and that's when the jealousy came about. Females hated to the point they would do anything to have Kenny drop me but he wasn't going for it.

After months went by I found out he was a thug and his name was banging in the streets of Grand Rapids. For a moment I always wondered how he received the money to purchase me nice gifts, buying expensive clothes and shoes and driving nice whips without me seeing any check stubs. He had me under the impression that he had a small low-key business until random people start coming around asking can they cop. I was use to money and material things because of my parents but not the fast life. I was so unsure about continuing our relationship but after a while of him proving to keep me safe I started to get comfortable because I knew he wouldn't let anything happen to me.

Snapping back into reality, I ended up calling Kenny again and I still didn't get an answer so I was planning on going straight home. Having a man that lived that fast life you had all kind of things going through your head when they didn't pick up the phone, you started thinking about them being in jail, being killed, cheating, or sleeping so I really didn't know what to think. That was my problem too, I always assumed the worst but when wrong been handed to you so many times you had no choice but to think badly.

Walking out the doors I was receiving a call from Lia, now she was the opposite of me but we still clicked from the very first day we met. She was loud, wild and crazy and I was sweet, innocent and shy. I had a little bad side but that barely came out, piss me off and I will set it off.

"Hey girl." I answered the phone sounding pissed off.

"What's wrong? She screamed through the phone. She always knew when something was wrong with me, she knew me like the back of her hand.

"Kenny ain't answering the phone bitch." I said rolling my eyes as if he was the one on my line.

"You need to me pull down on you so we can go handle him?" She laughed but sounding serious as hell.

"No. it's cool he's probably out just handling business." I said, but in the back of my mind I felt something wasn't right, and I swear I hated that feeling.

"Right. Well hit me back when you get home." She said and hung up.

I loved the relationship me and Lia had because she was always there for me, she wiped my tears when needed, held me when I cried and did anything else a best friend would do. She's been the same since day one and has never changed or switched up on me.

Once I got outside my job, I walked over to the car and jumped in. I was pushing an all-white Audi Q7. I loved my vehicle; it made me feel like a boss even on my worst days. Throwing on my MK sunglasses, I let my hair down from the wrapped up bun I had it in and drove off.

Driving down the street, I heard my phone beep letting me know I had a text message. Hoping it was Kenny I snatched the phone out my purse so fast that I nearly dropped it.

Bae: taking care of business boo. Be ready when I get home tonight. I love you.

Me: drive safe and you know I love you more.

That message from him had me smiling the entire ride home, not only because he texted me but I knew he was safe. Pulling into the drive way of our three bedroom three and a half bath home I parked the car and quickly ran inside. Our house was nice and comfortable for the both of us. The outside of our home was forest green and black, had huge windows and pretty green manicured grass, the best on our block if you asked me with a two stalled garage.

Walking inside the house, our living room was a modern theme with the colors of orange and brown. Everything in the living room was orange and brown; from the furniture, carpet, tables, and even the picture frames. The only thing that was black was our 60' inch flat screen T.V that was mounted on the wall.

The dining room just had a brown wood theme going on that followed the living room basic colors. Making my way through the house I stopped inside one of the guest rooms to turn off the television. We barely came inside these rooms so I don't know who would leave the T.V on. I had to remind myself to ask Kenny who was in our guest room when he comes home tonight.

Being that my man was coming home in about two hours, tonight I was planning on surprising him with something a little different. I always tried new things in the bedroom, because I would never want Kenny to feel like our sex life was boring.

15

The house was already clean, so that was something I didn't have to worry about. Walking into the kitchen I pulled out two wine glasses from the cabinet and reached below me to grab his favorite drink, which was Remy Martin. Our kitchen was different with a coffee crème tan and white color scheme. The countertops were white with chipped pieces of crème cracked inside the paint.

Looking at the time it was already midnight and he usually made it in around 1:00 or 1:30 no later than 2:00. My thoughts were interrupted with Lia calling me.

"Yes bitch?" I answered.

"Was everything good hoe?" She asked.

"Yea, girl it's cool. He will be here in about an hour or two."

"Um. Okay! Call me later." She said.

"Ok boo." I said hanging up.

Lia didn't really care for Kenny but she dealt with him because of me. With as much he'd put me through she felt like I deserved better; each time he cheated I always ran to her and then took him back, but that's what love will do to you. I knew Kenny didn't care for her much either. He always said she was ghetto and not the type of chick I should hang around. I didn't agree with putting a relationship before a friendship unless it was reasons. Lia was here before him and she wasn't just a friend to me, she was my family so I asked them both to get along with each other on the sake of me.

Quickly running inside our master bedroom, I walked inside the bathroom. I started to run me some bath water that I wanted to be real hot so I could relax my body for the night. Walking into the bathroom closet I got out some rose pedals and sprinkled them from the front door into the living room, to the sitting room and that will lead him into the bedroom.

***

Sitting in the tub soaking my body, it was now almost one o'clock. Washing my body with my Mad about You shower gel from Bath and Body works I made sure to take extra care in cleaning my sweet spots. To make things sexier I wanted to bring some strawberries and whip crème inside the bedroom with us.

Jumping out the tub, I dried off with my towel and walked into the room to get dressed. I looked inside my dresser and pulled out my brand new lingerie set Lia bought me for my birthday.

Applying lotion all over my body I slid on my thong and then put on the lingerie with it. Admiring my beauty in the mirror I was satisfied with how I looked because I knew I was the shit.

I was what these niggas called a "baddie" Standing at 5'7; my brown skin was smooth and had a gloss that you couldn't miss. Other bitches out here going broke just to get the natural jet-black hair I was born with. My hair was long and straight, with a nice shine to it. Not to mention, I had a body to kill for.

My stomach was flat and my ass was fattttt, my breast sat up perfectly so most times a bra wasn't necessary. I've heard a lot of people say I put you in the mind of Megan Good, but I was taller and had a much bigger ass.

Time was flying and there was no sign of Kenny walking in that door and I was now starting to get angry. I had everything looking nice for his arrival. I was lying in the bed in the middle of the rose pedals with the wine glasses sitting aside me with the drink between my legs.

He never came home after 2:00, and when I say never I really meant never. It was now 2:15 and he still wasn't home. I called and texted him and didn't get a reply, I was upset and sad at the same time because I had did all of this and my man wasn't lying next to me or fucking and sucking on me.

At this moment tears was falling from my eyes and I couldn't stop them. So, I just laid here and drank listening to the tunes of Tony Braxton. When will I ever learn? I asked myself.

Why did I continue to let him do the things he did to me. I was down for him, and even motivated him. These hoes he chasing around don't want nothing from him but his money but he's too blind to see it. I did everything for Kenny and still got treated bad. When he was slacking I was there to put him back on making sure he had enough money to flip, but just like a nigga once they get they clout back they get distance.

Any nigga would love to have a young beautiful girl like me. I didn't ask for much but honesty and loyalty. In my eyes, I could have anybody I wanted but I was too focused on Kenny trying to get him to change his ways even though it wasn't working. Any man would be lucky to run into a chick like me who stayed by his side, holding him down and not letting him down.

I never doubted my woman intuition because nine times out of ten I was always right. My mom always told me "Love would have brought you home last night" so therefore he can keep his black ass where he was staying.

Getting Kennys' foolish ways out my mind, I reached my hand underneath our king sized bed and grabbed my box full of toys. I kept this for times like this when I needed to relieve some pressure. It didn't satisfy me like Kenny would but it did enough. I know I am not the only chick who keeps things like this around. My excuse for having one was because of loneliness when Kenny wouldn't bring his ass home.

Laying my head back, I opened my legs and inserted my plastic dick and the vibration instantly had me gone. I played with my nipples and felt myself reaching my climax. Satisfied with my toy, I felt my juices run down the crack of my ass.

"It's always a plan B." I said to myself as I finished what was supposed to be Kenny's job.

Kenny

"Suck this dick girl." I groaned as shorty had her head bobbing up and down on my dick. She knew what she was doing when it came to satisfying me. I held on to her hair and began to fuck her face as if it was her pussy.

"Turn around." I demanded placing her on all fours. Once she assumed the position I rammed my dick inside her from the back. She was wet as hell, and the only thing you could here is her wetness and my balls smacking against her skin.

"Fuck me just like that daddy." She moaned out, twerking her ass on my dick.

"Shi-tt." I moaned as I unleashed my nut all on her ass. Once we finished we both got up and headed to the bathroom to clean ourselves up. This was something like my second home when Jasmine and I wasn't on good terms or when I just needed a quick nut. I would never make love to a thot the way I made love to my lady. Jasmine was the only one who got the real treatment.

I couldn't believe I was fucking up again but like a nigga I was just thinking with my dick and not my head. I knew soon as I got to the house Jasmine was gone be cursing my ass out and I really didn't have the energy to fight with her.

It was five in the morning and instead of me going home I just crashed at shorty house until I knew Jasmine was gone to work. She usually didn't go to work until seven so I had time to get me a nap in. I felt bad for the shit I put her through but sometimes a nigga needed a break from all that nagging. Since the miscarriage a couple years ago our relationship hasn't been the same. It seems as if Jasmine gets more insecure by the day and I hated that shit, and she always said I made her that way. Not wanting to leave her, I thought about the good's we had in our relationship. Jasmine thought losing the baby didn't affect me but in a lot of ways it did.

I was pissed that she hadn't told me before hand, and by the time I found out it was the same time we had lost the baby. I fucked around so many times that I had no clue as to who would want to harm her. To me, the shit wasn't that serious and I couldn't believe they took it that far.

I do shit that I know I shouldn't be doing, but I was a nigga and I couldn't help the fact that bitches wanted me. I'm not saying its okay for me to cheat but her complaining all the time and having them damn attitudes pushed me to fuck with other bitches.

The thing is when I cheat I'm not out looking for bitches that's fucking with my girl I'm out here fucking thots, bitches who got no respect for they self.

I'm not trying to come off cocky or no shit like that but I loved Jasmine and I would never put any female before her. She was my baby, yeah I knew she deserved better but I could never lay down and dream about her being in the arms of another nigga. Every nigga got that one female who they fall hard for, that one they gone bounce back with no matter what and who.

Once we finished in the bathroom I came into the room and grabbed my ringing phone off the dresser. Going through my apps I noticed I had millions of messages from Jasmine. I couldn't do nothing but laugh and shake my head.

One of the text messages said:

Wifey: I'm leaving and won't be coming back, I'm tired of you putting your side bitches before me. Fuck you and them hoes, they can have you because I damn sure don't want you. So by time you get here, me and my shit will be gone.

I couldn't and wouldn't lose my girl over no hoe so I had enough time to go home before she left, if she wasn't already gone.

The second message was a picture of our bedroom with some rose pedals, liquor and wine glasses on the bed with strawberries and whipped crème.

"Damn I'm fucking up." I said to myself. I guess you can't have your cake in eat it to. Even though we were going through some things, I didn't want to lose her. I had to learn how to be a man and realize what was in front of me. Because of my foolishness, my rock was walking out on me and I couldn't have that happen.

Jasmine was independent, educated and sophisticated. She knew she was the shit just by the way she walked and talked. I loved her because she was a good ass woman. When things weren't right she prayed for me, motivated me and kept me on my toes. She had a mind of her own and I liked that most about her.

"Yo, I'm out." I said throwing on my clothes and shoes.

"Where you going?" she said jumping out the bed.

"Home to my girl." I said looking at her side ways. Shorty had me fucked up if she thought I was gone sugarcoat the shit.

"Oh so now you running to the bitch? But when y'all have problems you over here fucking on me, That's for us now? You just gone leave me? What about us?" she snapped.

SMACK!

Before I knew it the back of my hand met her face. One thing I don't tolerate is disrespect towards my girl.

"Bitch play yo role, you knew we wasn't together. I don't owe you shit." I said walking out the door. Kema was now starting to act brand new, any other time she played her role the way I addressed it but now she was on some other shit.

I don't understand these side pieces, before they started fucking with you they already knew you had a woman and knew what was capable of happening. Being a side piece came with a lot of rules and choices but it was up to you to follow them, if you couldn't handle the heat then stay out the kitchen.

I can't lie, the money I had, the clothes I wore and the cars I drove is what attracted these hoes. Some I entertained and some I ditched. Growing up broke not getting attention from bad bitches I felt like the ugliest nigga around and once I got my money up and noticed the attention I was receiving I couldn't let them slip away even if all I did was wanted to bust a nut.

Pulling up to the house I had to think of a lie to tell Jasmine, of course I knew she knew what was happening but I couldn't just admit to her that I was out cheating, especially in her face.

Before I got out the car I sent my homeboy Twan a message letting him know if Jasmine contacted him to let her know I was with him at his crib all night. A couple times Twan told me he wasn't getting in the middle of me and Jas because he didn't want her to start hating him but at the end of the day he was my homeboy not hers.

Me: bro I need that favor again, wifey tripping.

The house looked dark so I didn't know if Jasmine was inside or not, and I couldn't see if her car was here because both garage doors were down. Once I got the OK from Twan I made my way to the side entrance of my home.

Twan: nigga, I told you I wasn't doing that shit no more lol. This my last fucking time helping you, keep yo dick in yo pants fool.

This nigga had his nerves. I got out the car making sure it was locked and walked up to the house towards the door. Everything inside the house looked the same, but I didn't hear any movement so I knew she wasn't home. It was 6:15 so she must have already left for work.

Running up the stairs to our master bedroom I was gone check her closet and dressers to see if she took her clothes out. When I got up there, I noticed some things off the top of her dresser were missing as far as her lotions and perfume sets. I knew all the sets she had because most of them I bought for her.

As I checked the closet for her bags and suit cases, I couldn't see anything. Once I turned the closet light on there was nothing inside here but my shit. FUCK! I knew I fucked up and let the only thing I loved slip away.

Walking around the room pacing back and forth I didn't know what else to do or say because I already knew it was over. I messed up too many times for us to be fixed. I was gone let her cool off and get the break she needed. I knew she wasn't gone far but over to her best friend Lia house. She always went there when things wasn't working with us. Being that Lia and Jas been friends since they was young I didn't want to come between their friendships but I couldn't stand Lia ass.

She wasn't the kind of female I wanted Jas hanging around, and sometimes it led me into thinking Jas was doing things with other nigga's behind my back. I was always told "birds of a feather flocked together" but Jas swore up and down she was nothing like Lia.

I wasn't always this disrespectful person I'm made out to be. When I lost my brother, my twin, my best friend I really didn't give a fuck about anything anymore.

Kevin was murdered right in front of me; his blood covered my clothes and bare skin. Seeing your sibling die in front of you was hurtful as hell. It was a drug deal gone wrong, and I never found the niggas that did it but I heard stories, many of them. My younger brother Moe always told me some shit about them East Side niggas doing it but I had no proof.

Kevin and Moe was all I had, my mom died of cancer and my dad died of a drug overdose but that didn't matter to me because when they was living they were already dead to me. They never gave a fuck about me. The streets raised me and taught me the shit I knew. I didn't feel the love I needed to feel from my father, the man who was supposed to teach me how to be a man. All I ever seen was an old junkie who spent his kids rent money to feed his nose.

My mom wasn't any better, whatever my father said went. Even when she got tired of doing drugs he made her do it just because he didn't want to get high by himself. My mom wasn't there to teach me how to respect and cherish a lady so I had no ways of knowing how. She was disrespected by my father so much to the point I thought that was the right thing to do, but I guess I was wrong. My father ended up leaving and that left my mom and us at the house. Months after he left we heard around the streets that he had overdosed and the police found him laying down at a park, while children was outside playing.

A couple of years after that, I ran into Jasmine back at the club. I made her mines and once we started to kick it more she agreed to move with me to help out with my mom while I was out getting money making sure they was taken care of. I never showed my mom any respect until her last days and that's what I regret the most because I waited until she got sick to be there for her when I should have done it when she was well. Even though she did what she did, she was till my mom.

I get in my feelings at times, what nigga don't? The shit I seen in my life I wasn't supposed to see, the shit I've heard I wasn't supposed to hear, especially being a youngin.

Looking over at Jas senior picture she kept on the night stand had me wanting to snatch her ass from work but in order me to do better I had to give her space.

If it wasn't for her giving me the money to get back on I wouldn't have the newest shit I got now. When I first met her I was heavy in the streets. My money was real long, but once those random ass East Side niggas came up, they took over the streets leaving my end dry as a bitch with wolf pussy. Broke or balling she was still there for me and that's the reason why I fucked with her the most. She never asked me for much and when I got back on and started bringing in a lot more money than I was, I made sure she was first on my list.

I got up and walked over to the table and started to roll me up a blunt before I hopped in the shower. Today I was putting everything behind me and focusing more on my money. Me and Twan had some things to get into later on.

Inhaling this exotic marijuana into my lungs I decided to send Jasmine a text, letting her know that I was sorry and wanted to take her out for lunch.

Me: Baby, I know your upset with me but I want to make it up to you. I really am sorry, I'm done coming in late nights and I'll be up there for your lunch break boo. Love you.

Hoping in the shower, I turned on the hot water and stood there allowing it run this sex scent off me from last night. I didn't give a fuck about my side piece feelings at all, Jasmine was my only concern. It wasn't like I led her on because I didn't, she knew I had a girl when she met me. And that's where most bitches fuck up at when they knew a nigga was in a relationship but think their pussy could be so good that a nigga would leave their main bitch. I couldn't do nothing but shake my head.

I heard a message come through my phone but at this very moment I really didn't feel like being bothered with anyone. I just needed to spark another blunt and let it ease my mind.

Once I washed my body I hopped out the shower and checked my phone. Seeing Kema's name in my notification bar I became aggravated, she always did shit like this. I don't understand what made her feel like she had tendency's to become my main when she knew she was my on call freak, I called her when I needed her.

Kema- Don't forget how grimy I can get boo. I can be a messy ass bitch considering I work with yo dumb ass broad. Or did you forget?

Jasmine

Work seemed to be going by so slow and I was beyond tired from sitting up half the night crying thinking my man was coming home to me. I couldn't even keep my eyes open; they were so heavy and red like I had been smoking a lot weed. Knowing Kenny, I knew the first thing he was gone check when he got home was my closet so I packed up a couple of things and put them into the trunk of my car. With the way my mind was set up last night my plans were to leave but something told me to do the opposite.

People say you never know what you have until it's gone, but that's not true, you knew that you had something good from the beginning but you didn't think you would lose it. The thing is with these niggas they feel like we gone sit around and wait for them to change and get their act together. Sometimes that's true but once a lady feels like she's done and had enough she will eventually get tired and leave his ass. No matter how much she loves him, she would have to learn to love him from a distance. Sometimes you have to put your feelings to the side and move on because life goes on whether you want it to or not.

Walking back to my cubical at work I looked down at my phone because it kept lighting up letting me know I had a missed notification. When I clicked the app my smile turned into a frown. It was Kenny texting me saying he's sorry like I didn't hear that shit thousands of times.

***

An hour later it was now time for my lunch break and I was heading to the break room to punch out on the time clock. Once I made it to the break room I noticed Kema was on the phone running her mouth to one of her messy home girls like always.

"Hey girl." She said smacking on a piece of gum. I hated to see a female chew like a damn cow that was so unlady like if you ask me.

"Hey." I spoke back.

"You brought lunch today?" she asked me.

"Girl naw, my man coming to take me out to lunch." I said as I finished punching in my identification number, that we used to clock in and out.

"Oh." She said dryly.

I didn't understand where her attitude came from all of a sudden but I really didn't care. I hope she didn't think I was gone sit in here and gossip about everybody in the city.

"Girl yeah, I fucked that nigga good as hell last night while his bitch was blowing up his phone." She said to whoever was on her other line.

I shook my head and walked out the room. Kema was messy and trifling as hell and I couldn't stand to be around her anymore. Things like that would piss me off when I knew my man had his hoeish ways.

As I walked to the front I was greeted by Kenny, who was holding a vase of fresh flowers. I smiled on the outside but in the inside I was still mad about last night. He can be a pain in the ass but he always knew how to cheer me up.

"These are for you baby." He said handing me my flowers.

"Thanks." I said rolling my eyes.

As we got ready to leave I heard someone calling my name and when I turned around I noticed it was Kema walking up to me.

"Girl my bad. Oh hello handsome, my name is Kema I'm one of Jasmine's friends." She smiled reaching out to shake Kenny's hand. I noticed Kenny didn't want to shake her hand but for what reason I didn't know why.

"Sup." He said back to her as he finally shook her hand.

"What's up Kema?" I asked rushing her to the point.

"I just wanted to ask if it was okay for me to use your computer until you come back because mines froze up again." She said patting her head, you know that pat you give your head when your weave starts itching bad.

"Girl I don't care, but let me go because you holding me up." I laughed. Kenny grabbed my hand and we walked out the door. I was gone ask him if he knew something about Kema that I didn't because the whole time I was talking to her the expression on his face wasn't good.

"You good?" I asked him noticing how his hands were gripping the steering wheel.

"Yeah, I'm cool." He lied.

If he was gone be acting like this then he can turn this truck around because I didn't have time for nobody attitudes especially when I had my own. I slid on a pair of my new Gucci Sunglasses and laid my head back. I kicked off my shoes and enjoyed the ride with the sunshine.

"I love you baby." He finally said. I looked over at him and wondered did he really mean it or was he saying it just to get back on my good side.

"Don't say anything you don't mean."

"What the fuck you mean? You know I love yo ass man." He yelled.

"Calm down, I'm just saying Kenny." I said rolling my eyes.

Pulling up to Beltline Bar, he parked his all-white 2015 Escalade truck and we got out. The parking lot was packed so I knew it was a mess inside. This place had the best burritos in Grand Rapids and I came here every time I got the chance to.

"Welcome to Beltline Bar, just you two?" Said the nerdy waitress.

"Yes it's just us." I said back. We walked to the back of the restaurant and sat down getting ready to order because I was beyond hungry. I always got The Famous Wet Burrito and large lemonade on the side.

"So you gone tell me where you were last night?" I asked him looking dead in his eyes. Studying his facial expressions I wanted to see if he was gone lie to me.

"Baby, I was out handling business with Twan, if you don't believe me you could call him right now." He said.

I wanted to believe him but then I couldn't. He has done so much shit I don't know when he was lying or telling the truth.

"If I find out anything, I'm killing you and the next bitch. Try me." I said moving my finger around in his face. He knew I wasn't about to call no damn Twan. That's his homeboy, so of course he gone agree to everything just to keep from getting his no good ass friend put out. Twan and I never got along so I don't even know why he suggested me to do that.

"I'm all yours ma." He said massaging my hands.

The waitress came to bring us our food and she didn't get a chance to sit it down because I was grabbing it from her hands. I was starving and it wasn't good that I drunk almost a fifth of

Remy Martin by myself last night, so yes my stomach was empty and this food was the only thing I needed.

As I looked at the clock it was now almost time for me to head back to work. I had exactly thirty minutes to make it. I finished drinking my lemonade and held small conversation with my man. Times like this was wonderful because we got to spend time together, something we didn't get to do often.

"I'm ready." I said wrapping up my food.

"Aight, let's bounce." He said as we got up. He left a hundred dollar bill to cover our food and the tip, then we made our way out the door.

Fifteen minutes later we was pulling up to my job and instead of him letting me out up front he parked far back in the parking lot.

"You really gone make me walk?" I asked with an attitude.

"Naw girl shut up and lay back." he demanded. I did as I was told and let the seat back so far that it was touching the back seats in the truck. Kenny was always on some freaky shit with me and I loved that side of him.

"You still mad at me bae?" he whispered in my ear, licking and sucking on my neck, as he used his free hands to pull down my loose work pants. I panted as I felt his fingers enter my wetness. Enjoying his touches I couldn't hold back anymore so I let my river run down his fingers.

"Just how I like it." He spoke as he stuck his fingers inside my mouth. Getting a taste of my own juices I smiled.

Kneeling down on the floor he gently lifted my legs up and ate his first and last meal of the day. I loved the fact that his truck had plenty of room. He slurped and licked on my pussy like the dehydrated person he was at the moment.

"Mmmhmm daddy." I moaned as he continued to suck me dry. Once he saw I was into it, he stopped and looked at me.

"You didn't say if you was mad or not?" he asked with a smirk on his face. I wanted to punch him in his fucking face. He kept sticking his fingers inside me and then he would take them out.

"I'm not." I answered. Once he heard me say I wasn't mad he finished doing his job.

"Shi-tt- I'm coming." I moaned out loud, grabbing a handful of his silky hair. Once I reached my climax, I pulled out some wipes I carried in my purse for times like this, because you never know.

"Have a good day at work." He winked his eye at me and smacked my ass as I got out the car.

As I made it back inside, I noticed one of the residents was heading out the door trying to escape. You were never supposed to leave them unattended, so somebody wasn't doing their job.

"Mr. Jenkins what are you doing?" I asked. When he heard my voice, he tried to roll faster in his wheel chair causing me to burst out laughing.

"Get away from me. I'm going home." He yelled.

"This is your home." I said, grabbing his chair to turn him back around.

Bringing him back into the nursing home, we were greeted by his nurse and one of the security ladies.

"He was trying to escape again?" asked his nurse.

"You already know huh?" I asked her.

After we got him to calm down I headed to my cubical to see who needed their medication. Working in a place like this you see things like that happening all the time. These elderly people were crazy and funny at the same time. They weren't in their right state of mind so we had no choice but to help them. Some of them understood us, but some of them didn't.

"Girl you smiling hard." Said Kema as she walked over to my desk with her 20 inch weave shedding all over my paperwork. I didn't even respond, I just looked at her and smiled harder.

The rest of my day was okay, I was heading over to Lia house so we could go to the salon and get our nails and toes done. I pulled up to her house and honked the horn waiting for her to come out. While I waited, I texted Kenny and asked him when was he going home because I knew if I wasn't coming straight home then he would eventually find something to get into.

"Hey bitchhhh." She said getting in the car.

"Heyy." I said back to her. We drove off and were on our way to the salon to have us a late night girls outing.

"So, what's new?" I asked her. Knowing Lia she always had something new to tell me about her and her niggas.

"Nothing this time girl, everything's the same." She said shocking the hell out of me.

Pulling in the parking lot of the salon we got out the car and made our way inside. It wasn't packed inside so it wouldn't take us anytime. Once we got inside, we took a seat and waited until someone was available. There wasn't a specific person I wanted to do my nails because they all did they thing, and each time I left I was satisfied.

Feeling my phone vibrate, I reached inside my purse and seen it was a message from Kenny.

Bae: Baby, what time you coming home? I'm bored and lonely.

Me: I didn't know you was home, but soon as I leave the nail salon I'll be there baby. It's kind of packed, but just wait love.

Bae: okay cool. Love you

Me: I love you more baby.

I just knew I was gone have to curse his ass out once I got home, but since he was already there waiting on me I didn't have to do all that. Tonight I just wanted to shower, relax and chill under my man and watch a few movies like old times, only if they don't end up watching us.

Kema

I was starting to get fed up with Kenny lying ass. For the past few years he's been telling me that we would make it official but its one thing that's stopping that from happening and it's his bitch ass girlfriend Jasmine. I've asked him several times why he needed her when he had me and he always preached that same line "I owe her my loyalty, and I love her". I was so tired of hearing that shit, I didn't understand what made her so different then me, why she deserved the wifey title when I did the same shit she did for him.

I cooked for Kenny, fucked him good and let him keep some of his drugs and pills in the basement of my house. I also had a job but for the wrong reasons, once I found out Jasmine worked at the Nursing Home around the corner from my house I took it upon myself and applied for the job just so I could keep up with their relationship.

This was the only job I've held in my life so I knew their wasn't a chance of me getting hired. I had no experience and once I found out I was getting interviewed by a man I did what I did best and sucked his dick for my Wellness Assistant position. The bad part about that now is he looks for me on the regular when I have my lunch breaks and sometimes called me outside of work and I was getting tired of sucking his little pink dick all the time. He threatened to fire me if I didn't continue and now I was at the point where I didn't give a fuck but I had to get in good with Jasmine to keep tabs on our nigga.

I know I sound stupid but I love Kenny's last year draws and I was tired of us being kept a secret when we did so much together, well behind closed doors. I really didn't know if the feelings were mutual between us but I knew he cared about me. I was willing to do anything just to have Kenny to myself. I was as grimy as it gets. I thought when she lost their child he wouldn't want to be with her anymore but the more he claimed to feel bad for her, the more he got closer to her. I needed my man to be home with me every day, not only when he needed to clear his head.

I got out the bed and quickly went to the bathroom to take care of my hygiene. It was later in the day so I had no plans at the moment but to get my nails fixed.

As I finished in the bathroom I got dressed and was out the door within seconds. Once I got outside, I got in the car and drove off.

I felt my stomach growling so I pulled into the parking lot of Judson's Steakhouse at the B.O.B to grab me a bite to eat. I turned the car off and walked inside, rushing so I can make it on time. I hated doing walk-ins because you had a longer wait.

"Welcome, would you be dining in with us today or is this take out?" The lady asked me at the front desk. Before I responded to her, I took a look at the menu that was posted behind her hanging on the wall. When I looked over to the left I heard a familiar laugh. I couldn't believe who the hell I was staring at.

"I'm sorry to waste your time, I won't be ordering anything." I said back. I wanted to hurry and leave before I get noticed, but I had to take pictures because now I got a plan that just might work out. I guess I wasn't the only one trying to be the only one.

Running out of the restaurant I got in my car and drove off heading to the Nail Salon. Tears were now starting to run down my face but I had to pull myself together in order for everything to flow right.

Sitting in the parking lot of Pleasant Nails & Spa I noticed Jasmine and another girl walking out sharing a laugh.

"Hey girl." I said jumping out the car. Even though I hated this bitch, Jasmine has always been a bad bitch to me, wasn't anything about her ugly, she was naturally beautiful. I wasn't a typical female, I mean I wasn't bad as Jasmine but I was beautiful with a banging ass body. My skin was on the darker side with a little gloss. My natural hair is shoulder length hair but I still chose to wear weave because it popped out more. I had full lips and stood 5 feet even.

"Hey." She spoke. Lord knows I wanted to kill her joyful spirit and show her the pictures of Kenny and his other chick that I seen him eating out with today, but I'll wait until I see her at work tomorrow. Just to save my own ass these pictures were the jackpot.

The vibration of my phone caught my attention and once I read the name my mood had suddenly changed.

"Hello?" I yelled through the phone.

"I need you." Said Mike, the hiring manager at my job.

"I'm doing something right now." I said with an attitude. I couldn't wait until this was done and over with. I didn't need a job this bad, in fact once Jasmine see these pictures I'm calling quits to all this shit. Fuck Mike and fuck this dam stressful ass job.

"Aw baby, when can you come over? My wife and kids are gone so I got the house to myself." He responded sounding like a baby.

"Give me a few minutes baby and I'll be on the way." I flirted back. I don't know what his wife called herself doing because he couldn't get enough of this black girl.

I was satisfied with my nails so I paid my tab and left the building. Heading over to Mike's house I texted him and told him I was on the way.

As soon as I got to his house he was standing outside on the front steps with a beer bottle in his hand with his shirt wide open showing his hairy chest. I didn't plan on being here longer than an hour, so I was coming to do what I was hired for.

"Come on because I have other shit to do." I said as we walked inside the house. I didn't want any of his nosey ass neighbors seeing me over here, it's bad enough I was having sex with this married man anyways.

"What's with the attitude sweetie?" he asked running his fingers through my hair. The touch of him, the sound of his voice all just annoyed me to the max.

"I got other shit on my mind." I snapped while I unbuckled his pants. I knew what would shut him up so I dropped my mouth down and went to work. I sucked and licked all around the tip so I could quickly get him to his peak.

"Mmmm, your skills are the truth." He admitted as he gripped the back of my neck.

"Yes they are." I replied back. Once I took all of him inside me I felt his body tense up letting me know his nut was coming. I rolled my eyes in irritation and played with his balls with my other hand, sucking on him like I was sucking on a Popsicle.

"Fu-ckk." He groaned out loud.

He released his load down inside my mouth and I got up and went to the bathroom to spit that shit right back out. I wasn't big on swallowing, only time I did it was when I was sucking on Kenny. I took my toothbrush and tooth paste out my purse and brushed my teeth. I had nice teeth and wasn't gone risk fucking these up.

"I'm about to leave Mike." I said gathering my things.

"Why so soon?" He asked running his fingers through my hair.

"I'm done doing what I came here to do, and like I said earlier I had other things to do. Plus, I'm sure your wife won't be gone forever." I said walking towards the door.

Once I came from inside the house, I got into my car and drove of blasting my Fetty Wap C.D. That nigga was fine as hell with his one eye. If I ran into him better believe I was gone bust it wide open for him, right on stage if he asked me to.

Pulling into my house, I parked the car and made my way inside. Once I walked into the living room Kenny was laying on the couch sleeping.

"Baby, why you didn't get in the bed?" I asked him.

"Shit, I couldn't make it. A nigga was tired. Cook me something to eat, I'm hungry as shit." He said wiping his eyes.

"What is it you want?

"It don't even matter." He replied back.

I walked into the kitchen to wash my hands and then I looked inside the cabinet to see what kind of sides I had that would go along with this chicken. I had no problem doing anything he said, because one day he will realize the kind of woman he had.

I overheard him laughing so I peeped inside the living room and noticed he was on the phone, with whom I didn't know. His body language and conversation told me he was talking to another bitch. Pissed off wasn't the word, so I walked into the living room, dropped to my knees and pulled his dick out his pants.

"I'll meet you there baby." He said, being so disrespectful.

Jasmine

It was another typical day at the work place and for some reason I wasn't tired and exhausted like I usually be so I prayed my day stayed like this. My spirt was happy and it felt good to actually smile more than cry, or worry.

My man and I were back on good terms and that's how I wanted them to stay. Yesterday when I came home after the nail salon he wasn't there but it wasn't too long before he pulled up. To tell the truth, as soon as I made it home and didn't see his truck I walked in the house and gave him a call and before I could snap he was pulling up in the drive-way.

Once he came inside the house he dropped shopping bags from different stores on the living room floor and ran me bath water, and after that we made love until the sun came up.

"Hey chick." Said Kema interrupting me as always.

"What's up?" I said back.

"I want to show you something." She said as she pulled out her phone.

I didn't know what the hell it was that she wanted to show me, but the way she was focusing on her phone it was something she really wanted me to see.

"I felt like you should know about this because it would be wrong of me to not say anything. Well yesterday I went to grab me a bite to eat and once I got inside I seen Kenny having dinner with another female." She spoke calmly. She handed me the phone and I just broke down in tears.

"Thank you." I said in the midst of a thousand tears. I was leaving him, I needed to get on with my life and get some space because I couldn't take any more of his foul ways. Here I am thinking everything was sweet but in reality he was still out here fucking around with the next bitch.

"We could find this bitch and beat the fuck out of her if you want to. Since I know you and how much you love him I couldn't just keep this from you." She said as she hugged me. I didn't understand why she was being over dramatic about the situation and we weren't even cool like that.

Ladies? When are we gone learn our worth and what we deserved? We let these men get the best of us and turn us into some crying machines.

I couldn't put up with this shit any longer; I needed time to focus back on me and getting myself together. What's meant to be will find its way if not, it is what it is. Lia always told me Never let a person see you sweat play they ass just like they play you. Any person hate when you do what they did to you. And one thing for sure is a nigga hate denial.

I'm not saying go out and be the hoe of the night, but walk around with your head held high like you just don't give a fuck. Even though you hurting inside let them see that you're smiling on the outside. We have to show these niggas that we don't fucking care about nothing anymore. Let them run back to us. From now on continue stacking your coins and let them entertain these hoes. I wasn't going to answer his phone calls, texts or anything.

I was loyal to the wrong somebody. I always told Lia I wished I was cold hearted like her but I knew someday a man would appreciate me the way I was and wouldn't expect any change from me.

After the conversation with Kema, we both went back to focusing on our work. Sitting down at my cubical at work I seen my phone light up and It was Kenny texting me saying he was on his way here to take me out for lunch again. Him thinking everything was cool between us when they weren't was bad on his part, playing that role like he so faithful.

I didn't want to see him, he did enough damage and I really don't think our relationship would ever be the same so this break I was giving him was well-needed.

Thirty minutes later it was time for my lunch and soon as I finished punching out I was walking to the entrance of the door. Before I got outside the doors, I spotted Kennys' truck pulling in the parking lot.

"Why didn't you reply to my message?" he said with a serious face.

"What do you want Kenny?" I asked sounding irritated by his company.

"What's the reason of the attitude ma? Damn, a nigga can't take his girl out for lunch anymore?" He asked licking his lips like he always did. He knew I would be running back, but this time I was going to show his ass better than I could tell him.

"Seems like you already did that." I said with an attitude, looking him dead in his eyes. Even though he was looking fresh and smelling good, I tried to not let that throw me off.

"Bae, what chu talking about?"

I laughed for a minute and pulled out my phone to show him what I was talking about. I had Kema send those pictures to my phone after she showed them to me.

"Mannnn. Where you get those from? You spying on me now?" He asked through gritted teeth.

"Bye Kenny. I'm done with you." I said trying to walk away from him but all he did was snatch me up by my arm, then he grabbed me by the back of my neck in a gentle way and dropped his tongue inside my throat.

"Stop Kenny, I'm not coming back home. We need a break." I finally said with tears in my eyes. I couldn't let him see me sweat, I had to put on my big girl panties and realize that shit happens all the times, it is what it is.

"A break? You wanna fuck with another nigga? You always trying to leave me and shit, just listen to me baby." He tried to grab my other arm but I pulled away from him.

"No, I just need time to get myself together and so do you." I said taking a deep breath sounding as confident as I needed to be.

"So this it for us Jasmine?"

"This is what you wanted. You out here fucking with these dusty hoes not caring about me. You don't need me." I said calmly.

"Cool, I'll give you a break but if I hear anything about you fucking another nigga out here, I'll kill you and him, now play with me." He said walking off.

"WHATEVER." I yelled getting into the car.

I slid on a pair of my Gucci Sunglasses and sped off leaving him there to do nothing but stare at the back of my car. Inserting my K Michelle C.D I let her sing You can't Raise a Man to me as if she made this song personally for me.

Kenny was never gone grow up and become a real man. He was worried about the fast life and bad bitches but once his money gone those same bitches he was entertaining ain't gone want or need his ass anymore.

Pulling up to Subway I got out the car and walked inside, since I was the only one here I knew there would be no wait for me to order my food. Instead of me taking my sub to go, I decided to stay here and eat so I wouldn't have to eat and drive.

Feeling my phone vibrate inside my purse, I reached in and pulled it out noticing somebody was blowing me up. Looking at the name I had several texts from Kenny, and the first one I noticed read.

Bae: let me find out you going to meet yo nigga, you think I'm playing with you Jas. I'll kill you before you let any nigga between them legs.

His message didn't frighten me one bit, yes he was crazy but I could get crazier if it came down to it. Once I finished my food, I walked out and headed back to work. I had exactly two hours left and I was gone be heading to Lia's house.

As I made it back to work I walked inside and heard a lot of yelling and screaming. I got to the lobby and seen Kema and Mike fussing at each other.

"Girl calm down before you lose your job." I said to her soon as I got her attention.

"Fuck this job." She said snatching away from me walking out the doors.

I never seen Mike act like this so it had to be something serious going on and I couldn't wait to find out. Working here all the girls gossiped so it was going to get around the job sooner than later.

***

It's been three months since the last time I saw Kenny, he called and texted me several times but I ignored them each time. Today me and Lia were out shopping and decided to have ice-cream. I was looking good in my all-white summer dress with the back out, and my white MK sandals and purse to match. I ended up going to the salon getting my hair straightened so now it was hanging down my back with a middle part.

"Roll up hoe." Said Lia, she couldn't go a day without smoking.

"You a weed head." I said rolling my eyes at her.

"Sure is, my man ain't complaining. We smoke and fuck all dayyyy." She replied back sticking her tongue out.

"Which one?" I asked with one eyebrow lifted up. You needed a notebook to keep up with Lia and her niggas.

"Fuck you."

I wasn't a smoker but being with Kenny he insisted that I learned how to roll up his weed for him. It took me a long time to actually learn how to do it but once I learned I had it down pack. I hated the way weed smelled on my fingers but anything to satisfy him I did it.

Pulling into the Rivertown Mall it was cars everywhere so that told us it was a crowded inside. It was a beautiful day and since we lived in Michigan we had to appreciate and take advantage of days like this because our weather was so bi-polar.

"Damn why she staring that hard?" asked Lia.

I followed her eyes and noticed some chick was staring us up and down but I didn't know her from a can of paint. She was real cute, I always gave credit when it's due. I'll never be a hater. Once I saw her full face I had to double look because she looked familiar to me.

"I don't know her but don't start nothing today hoe, we cute and just got our nails done. Not today! We will not let these hoes mess up our cuteness." I giggled even though I knew she wasn't gone agree. We could never go anywhere without her finding some reason to smack a chick.

"You right but she better look the other way before I fuck her up." She snapped.

Walking into Bath & Body Works I was looking for some new scents that just came in but they really didn't have any so I ended up grabbing me some more Forever Red, which happened to be one of Kenny's favorite.

Hours later I started to get tired, the fact that we went into every store and plus my stomach was growling like crazy. Too many people were coming in, and I hated when someone bumped into me and not excuse themselves. When Lia shopped she doesn't know how to skip a couple of stores or two, she had to stop into every store located in the mall.

"We need to go to the city next time." I said, sounding irritated. Our mall never had anything, everything was old or too many people had it already.

"I agree." she said back.

Walking through the food court we were heading out the door. When I looked up towards the other side of the inside doors I noticed Kenny was coming in. Part of me wanted to speak but part of me wanted to keep walking. I missed him like crazy but I couldn't let him see it. "Fuck, he just had to walk over here by me" I said to myself.

"You can't speak?" he asked. He was looking good as always. His braids were freshly done and the smell of his Gucci cologne stuffed my nose.

"Hey Kenny." I said with an attitude.

"How you been?"

"Good and you?" I asked, sounding like I was ready for this conversation to be over already.

"I been straight, I miss you."

My heart dropped and I just stared at him not knowing what to say back. Yes, I missed him but I had to play it cool. I kept staring at him, searching for answers to the questions I had. Like, why did you do me the way you did? Was I not enough for you? Just why?

"Look enough is enough girl, stop trying to play that role like you don't miss me and shit. You were thinking about me just like I was thinking about you. I know I fucked up and made some mistakes but I'm only human and I learned from every one of them. Come back when you ready, but don't keep me waiting too long. "

"Girl come on, shit it's hot as hell and you got me sitting out here in the damn car." Lia said interrupting us, purposely.

"Look I got to go." I said walking off. I had to continue my journey of remembering how to function without him.

"Remember what I said."

Was he serious this time? Did he really change? Is he going to do right by me? I wish I had someone to answer these questions besides my heart. My heart was telling me to take my ass back home but my mind was telling me to stay my ass right where I was.

"Girl go home to your man." Said Lia as we got into the car.

"What if he ends up doing the wrong shit again to me?" I asked.

"That's when you kill his ass." She laughed not finding me serious.

"I'm serious Lia."

"Look boo, if you think you're ready then go but if not then you can stay. Follow your heart." She said. She was the last person to give out advice so I don't even know why I asked her coldhearted ass.

That's the thing my heart always led me into running back to him and then he do something to fuck it up again. I just wish everything would go back to normal, but with so many heartaches and heartbreaks I knew it would never be the same.

The ride back to her house was silent; I couldn't get my mind off Kenny and the things he said to me. I can't lie, I been horny so much lately and my fingers or toys wasn't giving me the real satisfaction that I needed so maybe I should go back home, but maybe I shouldn't because now I'm just letting sex answer for me and that's one of the reasons why I'm always running back.

We made it to Lia house and we grabbed our bags and headed inside. Once we settled in the house Lia asked me if I wanted to drink and I told her yes.

Lia made her way over with some liquor and tonight I just wanted to get my mind off Kenny. Whoever said you couldn't have fun at home lied, we were the true definition of that.

"You know what's crazy best friend?" she asked me sounding so serious.

"You?" I laughed.

"That too, but how good dick never comes from a good nigga. It's always them niggas who get an innocent girl and fuck her life over. The ones who always lying and cheating, getting rentals every week, drinking lean, smoking weed and have millions of hoes. But then you don't want a nigga who can't satisfy your needs, but I bet you he won't be cheating." She sounded so serious. I just looked at her.

"You crazy as hell for that." I said gulping my drink down and dancing to Keyshia Cole.

It's been a while since we got together and did this, either we were working or just handling business like women do. Its times when you won't always get to see your best friend but when you're grown and have responsibilities you should know where your friendship stands with one another. But once you get together, you laugh, cry, and do everything friends do and that's why I loved Lia crazy ass.

The more this Hennessey got into my system the more I started to reminisce on all the things me and Kenny did in the bedroom. He's the only guy to knew how I loved to be kissed on my neck and thighs, how I liked my nipples sucked. He knew everything about me from the good and bad.

When I felt the warmth down below I knew it was time to put this drink down because if I didn't, I was gone end up making a puddle on Lia's furniture.

***

The next morning I woke up with a hangover knowing I had to be to work in two more hours. I got up and headed to the bathroom but first I wanted to peek in Lia room and see if she was up. Soon as I got by her door I noticed she had her DO NOT DISTURB sign up so I knew she had some nigga up in there because that's the only time that sign goes up. I had to be knocked out to not hear him come in here last night.

I walked in the bathroom brushed my teeth, and washed my face and started to run me some bath water until I heard a door close. I opened the bathroom door and peeked out the little crack.

I seen some dark skin dude with dreads heading out the front door. I never seen him before so he had to be a newbie.

"This hoe." I mumbled under my breath.

Sitting in the tub I was relaxing my body until Lia burst inside not knocking or nothing. She always did this and didn't care about me being naked.

"Damn bitch I could have been playing with the kitty or something." I laughed.

"That's yo lonely ass, I got me some last night. Hell, my kitty needs a rest." She chuckled.

I just looked at her and burst out laughing because she didn't care what came out her mouth.

Sitting in the tub I had numerous things on my mind. The water felt so good and hot against my body. I knew I was going back to him but I had to make sure I was ready, and I needed him to see that I wasn't up with playing his games anymore.

We're grown and I shouldn't have to keep reminding a grown ass man what he's supposed to do and what he shouldn't be out here doing, and entertaining other bitches was one of them.

Jasmine

Another month went by and I decided to go back home and hopefully things with Kenny would be different. I had every right to our home just as well as he did, so I didn't need a time for my arrival. Those months without Kenny were hard on me but I got through them. I've never been away from him that long and hopefully I wouldn't have to leave him anytime soon.

Time had flew by so fast without me even knowing it. I was already walking out the doors on my way home from work. This morning I put my things into my car when I was leaving Lia house. I knew she would miss me, but I'll be seeing her soon.

Before going home, I decided to stop by the grocery store and pick up something for dinner tonight. I had my mind on some pork chops, salad, garlic bread and lasagna. This was Kenny's favorite meal, so I knew he would love for me to come back home being so he probably hadn't had a good home cooked meal like mines since I left him.

Pulling up to the supermarket, I grabbed my purse and jumped out the car heading into the store. Those ten hours had my feet swollen like I was a pregnant chick and I couldn't wait to get home and have Kenny massage them.

I was running through these aisles like I had lost my mind hoping I didn't forget anything I needed.

I made it back to the car, making sure I didn't leave anything in this basket because I wouldn't be coming back to the store if I did. I hated grocery shopping but having a man in the house who ate like a pig you had no choice but to keep food around.

Driving down the street I tried calling his phone to see if he was at the house but I didn't get an answer. I just needed him to help me bring the bags in because my arms and back was so sore.

I pulled up to the house getting myself together. I sat there for a moment taking a deep breath, making sure this was the right decision or what not.

I quickly got out the car, grabbing the bags with both hands, I then closed both doors. My hands were hurting so bad. I'd been lifting old people around all damn day and now I'm carrying ten heavy ass bags.

Walking up towards the garage I could see that his car was in the drive way so I knew he was here. Knowing him he was probably sleeping or in the shower and had his phone on vibrate.

I walked inside the house and everything looked normal so I peeked inside the living room and dining room and didn't see anything out of place. I missed being home so much, the smell was so delightful.

Stepping towards the stairs I could have sworn I heard movement coming from one of the bedroom beds up stairs. I stopped for a second and said to myself DON'T ASSUME GIRL, DON'T ASSUME.

When I got closer I heard moaning coming from the bedroom. Dropping the bags in the kitchen, I started to walk up the stairs quietly.

I reached my hand into my pocket and sent Lia an emergency text because I was sure someone was up here fucking. I didn't know if it was coming from our bedroom or the guest bedrooms.

"I know dam well this nigga ain't fucking in the house we share." I said running up the stairs. My heart was pounding, my mind was racing and my body was tremendously shaking.

Good thing our stairs had carpet, I pulled my gun out my purse and soon as I got closer to the bedroom I could hear the moans coming from our master bedroom. Peeking through the crack of the door all I could see was a bitch on top of him.

"What the fuck?" I yelled with tears running down my face. There was nothing I could do or say anymore. I came home thinking this nigga had changed his ways, thinking he was ready to build something together. But I was wrong, wrong about everything.

The sight of walking in on your boyfriend fucking another bitch in your house was heartbreaking and embarrassing. I never thought I would see anything like this, but boy did he prove me wrong. I was tired, and enough was ENOUGH. I had put up with too many females and this time I was done. He's always chosen the next bitch over me and I was done with him for real because he had me all the way fucked up if he thought we could fix this, not this time. So many times I said I was done with him, but this was the last time those words would leave out my mouth. I deserved better from someone who knew how to love and appreciate a good woman.

"Baby I'm sorry." He yelled.

I locked the door and just stood there in shock. Deep down inside I was hurt. At this very moment I didn't know what I was capable of doing. Shit like this is what drives a bitch physco and I was ten seconds away from tearing this house down.

"This for us?" I sked with the gun pointed at him.

"Jas put that fucking gun down." He shouted.

She was a pretty ass girl too, so I couldn't even say he downgraded. She was a caramel skin chick who had a big booty, thick thighs, her waist was slim and had no stomach standing at least 5 feet and 2 inches. What did she have that I didn't?

"Do I know you?" I asked, looking at her familiar face.

"Do you?" she laughed.

Once she smirked it hit me, this was the same bitch on the pictures Kema showed me, which is the same chick who stared us down at the mall, so that explains why she was looking so hard she knew all about me when I didn't know shit about her. Who did this bitch think she was? Did she not see this gun in my hand and she got the nerves to get smart, and then laugh at me like I was a joke.

"Bitch what's going on?" asked Lia breaking into the room with her gun in her hand.

That's what I loved about her down ass, she was ready for anything and if I told her the location of where I was going and she didn't hear from me in ten minutes she was already on her way ready for war.

"You know I don't miss out on shit." she said.

All I could do was stare at Kenny, I wanted him to see the pain in my eyes. Why didn't he fucking care? Why did he want me to come back?

"Shoot her ass or I will." Demanded Lia.

"Over some dick?" the girl asked.

"You damn right, some dick that don't belong to you." Lia snapped.

Taking my eyes off them, I turned and looked at Lia letting her know we was ten seconds away from fucking some shit up.

"BESTIE WATCH OUT." Lia yelled.

POW! POW!

I shot Kenny twice in his shoulder but my intentions weren't to kill him. I wanted him to feel the pain I felt from all the things he done to me. He fell down to the ground while the girl was standing in the corner looking stupid.

Lia was telling me to watch out because Kenny was coming in my direction.

"Bitch, I swear if I live to see another day I'm killing yo ass." He yelled, screaming from the pain that his arm was causing him.

We both were focused on Kenny and I knew he kept guns around the room but I didn't know if he moved them or not because I haven't been here in a while.

POW! POW!

The bitch shot but missed, thank God. I took a deep breath and released my bullets like a champ. I wasn't planning on killing neither one of them, but when she shot her gun I had no choice. I had my gun out just to scare her, but this chick was hard core.

POW! POW! POW!

Once I saw her body lying across the bed full of blood. I looked at Kenny and shook my head leaving him here for dead; we ran down the stairs and grabbed everything that had my name on it which I kept in a small box in the closet. This what he wanted? A crazy bitch? Well he got it, rest his soul and hers.

"Hurry up bitch." Said Lia.

"I can't just leave him up there like that." I cried.

"Fuck him." She said.

Soon as we got outside we both got in our cars and I followed her. The whole time I was driving, I was crying, banging my hands against the steering wheel. My hair was all over my head looking like a wild junkie or something.

It's true a man gone only do what you allow him to and that's how I looked at me and his relationship. He kept doing what he was doing because he knew I was in love with him and no matter what he did to me I was gone end up taking him back whether it was months or weeks later. I was in love, deep in love to the point where nothing or nobody mattered to me when it came to him.

Numerous times I caught bitches texting his phone saying they was burning, thought they was pregnant and all kind of different shit. Well as of today, I was a single woman not looking for love or attention; I'm just gone focus on me and continue to stack my money.

It was nothing for me to get another house I had money so that was never an issue in my life. Making it to Lia house I took a deep breath and thought about what I had just done.

Before I got out the car I stopped and paused and asked myself is he dead? Did I kill him? What the fuck did I do? Should I go back? Lia didn't let the shit phase her one bit, running around like we didn't have two bodies on our hands now.

Millions of questions were going through my head, but all I wanted to do was chill, drink and cry myself to sleep knowing that Lia wouldn't let that happen. She lived her life acting like she had no care in the world.

"You gone be okay boo." She said.

"I'm not." I cried.

I couldn't even enjoy my drink like I wanted to; all I wanted to do was cry and sleep my life away. How could he be so careless? How couldn't he see that he found him something good? Thousands of questions ran through my head as much I tried getting him out my mind it wasn't working.

"You deserve better queen." Lia said walking over to me to console me letting me flood her chest with tears.

I wanted this to be the last time I cried over the same situation so I was letting everything out.

"Thanks for letting me stay here bestie." I said wiping my face. She looked at me as if what I said bothered her.

"Now you know this is your second home." She said pouring us another drink.

"Yeah I don't know what I was thinking." I responded back. I was starting to feel better but because of what happened I was still frightened and worried about what was going to happen next.

Slim

Three years later......

I was a free man, those three years had a nigga stressing but I handled my shit like I was supposed to and did the time since I did the crime. Walking out the door I was smiling from ear to ear, I was ready to be back home and get on my money shit without the beef. Now, I looked at things differently and wanted to make money the right way. I earned my money illegally but that was the end of that.

Sitting in the parking lot I was waiting on my homeboy Rock to come get me, this nigga was known for being late so I might as well get comfortable. This was my last time seeing this place and I had no intentions on coming back here. I didn't want to live my life dodging the police anymore, and I wanted strangers to feel comfortable and safe around me not scared.

I heard a horn beep twice and when I turned around I was looking in the eyes of my day one nigga.

"My nigga." He said, dapping me up.

"You know it. What's been good boy?" I asked hoping in the car.

"Same shit, you ready to make some money?" he asked.

"I think I want to do something different now." I said.

"What you mean nigga?" he asked.

"I'm gone still make my money but the right and legal way. I got more than enough money saved up to do what I want." I said sounding serious.

"When you decide this?" he asked looking curios.

"Since I lost Princess." I said.

"Word? I'm down but you know the streets are all I know." He said.

"I know that nigga, I don't expect for you to change your lifestyle just because I did. We two different dudes and now we got two different hustles. " I said.

"The king turning in his crown." He laughed.

"Yeah nigga, it's a new me. Where Moe ass at?" I asked.

"Somewhere fucking another nigga bitch." He said.

"That nigga ain't gone never change." I said.

Rock was my right hand man one of the only niggas I did business with besides Moe. Me and his relationship was way different then mines and Moe. I trusted Rock with my life, and never did he fuck me over. We been getting money together since we was youngins, both running around the hood in some Walmart clothes, and some payless shoes until we jumped on the money team.

Moe was different, he was careless and greedy. Our relationship wasn't too bad and it wasn't too good. He only wanted to make money to be seen and stunt. I knew this nigga was gone have something to say about me leaving the streets but I didn't give a fuck how anybody felt.

Back then, before I got locked up I came in prison with a different attitude and that Slim would have got out ready for war but the Slim I am today, the Slim that decided to take life more seriously. I got tired of bagging up work, breaking it down and cooking it. Enough was enough, and I was gone prove it to everybody that it's more to life than that.

Yes! The money was quick and easy but we never stooped and thought about our life and freedom. Prison didn't make me a coward, it just made me smarter.

I graduated from high school and college, but doing the wrong things fucked my life up. I wasn't with the working a 9-5 and damn sure couldn't sit around waiting for a pay check so hustling was something I became addicted to.

I earned my degree in business and I was planning on making something happen with that degree because I feared jobs turning me down because of my past, so I wanted to buy some old buildings that were decent, fix them up and start me a restaurant and club and also something for the teenagers to enjoy.

I wanted something like a big youth center, a place where they can come out and get away from home if they needed to. Children who wanted to do something with their lives. Inside my youth center I wanted a study room for those who had homework or needed to study. The age limit was going to be 10-18. I didn't want anything above 18 knowing they were gone come in and try to take over.

Pulling up to my crib everything looked the same, I knew my nigga Rock was holding shit down for me and holding on to my money. Money wasn't a problem for me, and you could never make enough of it.

"Call me once you get situated nigga." Said Rock.

"Bet." I said getting out the car.

Walking inside my house I couldn't stop smiling. Everything looked the same like I had just left yesterday. Only thing that was missing was my baby Princess. Three months after I got locked up I got the news she was murdered, that shit fucked my head up because she was the only woman I grew to love besides my mom. Together for three years, I never thought we would have made it that far because we were too much alike but timing proved me wrong. I wasn't ready for a new relationship I was just on some stacking my money type of shit. If luck brought me in the arms of another woman I promise to never let my past bring us misery.

Many nights I found myself in my cell shedding tears. Nobody would ever understand the love we shared or the shit we been through. That girl had the key to my heart she was my queen and I was her king. The last time she came to visit me I could tell some things was on her mind because our conversation wasn't the same. Usually she talked about how happy she was to see me and how she missed me but those words never left her mouth, and that was the last time I had seen her.

Shit sure did change, she stopped accepting my calls, I wasn't a selfish nigga I always told her if she felt like three years was a lot to her then she didn't have to wait on me but at least pretend to care about a nigga. Being locked up all a real nigga wanted and needed is some attention because I know how shit went, I didn't care about you fucking with somebody else but at least keep writing me, accepting my calls and making sure I'm straight.

We were like Bonnie and Clyde, every hood nigga needed that hood bitch and that she was. She made sure I had money on my accounts, came and visit me whenever she could but within that month things started to change about her. When you been with someone for some years, you grow to know everything about them.

She was hard core and I was in love with her. Princess had Caramel skin with a juicy booty, thick thighs with a slim waist and stood at 5 feet even. She was young, street smart and educated and had beauty and brains, a woman every man needed. I never talked about her to anyone because I felt that her death was my fault, so I've been blaming myself. When Rock came to visit me and he told me about her death, I dropped tears because nobody would ever understand what we had and I would never love another bitch the way I loved her. She was my rock and kept a nigga on his square. Thinking about her, I started to reminisce on the first day we met.

It was a night at the bar, I had just got done taking my mom out to dinner for Mother's day and after I dropped her off at home I decided to go have me a couple of drinks. I walked inside and she was the first thing I laid my eyes on. Her smile is what caught my attention, because she had the perfect white teeth that I had ever seen on a female.

"Hey, how you doing Miss Lady?" I said.

"I'm doing good sir, and yourself?"

"I'm good; excuse my rudeness Happy Mother's day." I said, to see if she had a baby daddy or not.

"Oh, no I don't have any kids." She laughed.

"Oh cool, just didn't know if you did or not." I said.

"I understand." She said.

"You should let me take you out sometime." I said admiring her beauty and figure.

"That's cool, here's my number call me." she said writing her number down on my hand.

"Aright, I'll call you." I said.

Watching her walk away I'd never seen something so beautiful, until I laid eyes on her. She was everything to me.

Snapping me out my thoughts I was receiving a call from my mom and if I didn't answer this call she was gone curse my black ass out.

"Hello beautiful." I said answering the phone.

"Don't hello beautiful me, you wasn't gone call me?" She snapped through the phone.

"Yeah ma, I just got in the house. How you and pops doing?" I asked.

"We doing well, now you stay your ass out of there." She said.

"I will, I'll be by to see y'all and I love y'all." I said.

"We love you more." She said hanging up the phone.

Growing up life wasn't all good and it wasn't all bad either, I didn't have everything I wanted but my parents made sure I had what I needed. I didn't wear the finest clothes but they were clean, I didn't have the Jordan's, Nikes or Samoa's on my feet but they made sure my feet weren't bare. I wanted more and needed more. I'm not saying I didn't appreciate what my parents did for me because I did; I just wanted to match everybody else fly.

They worked their asses off to provide for me and my sister, but after she was born things were different with her. I was older then and made my own money because I was never gone have my sister out here looking ratchet. I made sure she had the newest clothes that came out, the newest Jordan's and her hair stayed done every two to three weeks. Growing up in Muskegon, everything was a competition so I couldn't sit and watch my sister come home crying saying people talked about her.

Damn! I missed my baby sis so much, I felt like she didn't even get a chance to live in this bull shit ass thing called life. I was fucked up in the head, because I didn't only blame myself for Princess' Death, I blamed myself for my baby sisters' death to.

She was killed in a drive by because some punk ass niggas had the balls to bring they're beef to the crib where we laid our head at and since then me and my father's relationship wasn't the same. This shit happened a year before I got locked up and things ain't been right since then. My father would speak to me when he seen me but nothing more than that. We didn't have those father and sons conversations we use to have when I came over to the house, he didn't ask me to join him when he wanted to go fishing or when he wanted to go have a drink and shoot pool he never thought about dialing my number and I missed the hell out of that.

Standing in my room looking for something to wear I pulled out some basketball shorts and a white tee because I wasn't planning on getting out the house today. Walking into the bathroom, I looked in the mirror and smiled like a lil ass kid. Why? It felt good to be out of prison and not only was I happy to be home I had business to attend to, as in getting things right with my restaurant, club and youth center.

Getting ready to take care of my hygiene, I brushed my teeth, washed my face, and then hopped in the shower.

Standing in the shower, I started to think about the exact day I got locked up. I had a lot of minor charges so I didn't know how much they was gone throw at my ass, but luckily I ended up with only three years.

Tonight was a night we were going out with Rock and his girl. We was what people called a power couple, everybody wanted to be like us, and everywhere we went we had haters because all we did was dress to impress.

It was a night to remember, me and Princess had got dressed and decided to go out and have fun.

"Baby girl you looking nice." I said looking at her clothing.

"Thanks King, you looking good yourself." She said back.

We pulled up to this spot called Nubby's this was a tight spot where everybody come out to enjoy themselves. We walked in and all eyes were on us, having a nigga feel like he was a celebrity or something. So many bitches tried throwing pussy at me, I fucked around a couple times but nothing serious to fuck up what I had at home.

It was people all over the place was looking good from top to bottom. I kept noticing some random nigga who I had never seen before kept watching me and following my every move but I didn't react to it because it was nothing serious.

We walked in and sat down in the back of the club making sure I was in a position to keep an eye on everything. When something wasn't right I didn't make a scene because I didn't like doing shit when my girl was around.

I got up to go to the bathroom to make sure I wasn't tripping about how this nigga kept watching me. I felt something was gone go down that night but I didn't say anything because I never was the type to make a scene first, and I dammed sure didn't want Princess there while the bull was going on. I made my way to the bathroom, and looked at dude out the corner of my eye, and I noticed dude watched me the entire time I came out the bathroom.

What the fuck up with this clown ass nigga? I thought to myself.

I kept thinking about how I was gone get Princess out the club before shit got real. I made it back to my seat and noticed the nigga wasn't standing there no more.

"What's wrong king, you look all worried and shit." Said Princess.

"Everything good baby girl, we gone be heading out in a minute though." I said back cutting the conversation short.

Princess had a confused look on her face because she knew something was up with me, we had just gotten there about 30 minutes ago and I was already ready to bounce.

"Look baby, if something's up let me know so I can be prepared, because you and all these bitches in here know I'm ready and down for anything." she said taking her heels off.

"Everything good and you know I don't like you wrapped up in any kind of bull shit anyway." I said back.

I texted Rock and Moe and told them to meet me by the entrance because of that gut feeling I had.

"What's good?" Asked Rock.

"I feel like some shit gone go on, but you know I'm not worried and you know I don't want Princess in here if it do, so just keep yo eyes open."

"You know we got you G, ain't shit gone happen to us or Princess." He said.

Soon as I sat down at the table, I heard bullets flying around our heads, I threw Princess down under the table.

POW! POW! POW!

"Blast back nigga, blast back." I said.

All I was thinking about was trying to get Princess out of the club, and make sure we all came out alive. I start blasting my pistol at the same time trying to make it over to Princess, but when I turned around I had to take a double look because I noticed she pulled out a gun out of her tote bag and start shooting with me.

Only thing I was thinking is when and where the hell she got that from. Bullets were flying everywhere and bodies were dropping like crazy. All you heard was gun shots coming from all directions.

Finally, I made it over to her shooting back towards the people who was shooting we made it out the club and jumped in the car. I looked back to see if Rock was behind me and soon as I turned around I saw him pulling up on the side of me.

"Y'all straight nigga?" he asked.

"Always, get the fuck out of here bro." I said making sure he left before me.

Speeding off in the parking lot I was putting my gun inside my glove compartment and soon as I turned the corner I saw lights flashing through my review mirrors.

"Fuck." I yelled.

"Hell naw." She said.

I pulled over to the side of the street and had Princess get my insurance and registration papers from the glove compartment before the police come to the car.

"License and registration please," He said flashing the light.

"Here you go sir and can I ask you what I'm being pulled over for?" I asked.

"Do you know you were speeding, the speed limit is 55 and you were doing 70" He said.

"I didn't even pay attention sir, I'm sorry." I said.

He went back to the car and I already knew I was fucked because of the small charges I had against me.

"Baby if they take my ass you already know wassup." I said.

"Slim don't talk like that, we straight." She said sounding nervous.

"Sir you have a couple of warrants, I'm going to ask you to step out the car." He said.

Soon as I got out the car, another police was pulling up behind us, I already knew so I just said fuck it.

They asked Princess to get out the car so they could search my car, for what reason I didn't know. Soon as he went to the front seat he searched everything and removed my gun from my glove department. I didn't argue, I didn't shake my head I was a street nigga and I knew the consequences.

"Sir does this gun belongs to you?" he asked.

"Yup." I said back.

On his way walking towards me, I looked at Princess; she didn't look scared or worried because she already knew how the game went.

"I love you King." She said getting inside the police car.

"I love you too ma." I said.

Hopping out the shower to a ringing phone, I looked at the name and saw it was Moe ass calling me. I knew he was gone be talking shit, because that's all his ass did.

"Talk to me." I said answering the phone.

"I see you out nigga, let's get back to this money like the old days." He said.

"I'm on some different shit now bro." I said.

"Like what?" he asked.

"I'm done with that street life." I said.

"How can you be done? You the king of this shit." he laughed.

"We'll talk more bro." I said.

"Bet." He said as he hung up.

Rushing into my room I threw on my clothes and applied my lotion, deodorant and Gucci cologne. As I got dressed my stomach started to growl, I need some good ass food.

Searching through the kitchen draw I pulled out some menus to the Chinese place up the street and I was ready to order up some shit. To me you couldn't think on an empty stomach. I got tired of eating that damn prison food but as the days got longer I got used to it.

"Hello. What could I get for you?" asked the lady on the phone.

"Could I get 6 crab ra-goons, large shrimp fried rice, three egg rolls and some duck sauce." I said rubbing my stomach.

"Would that be all for you sir?" she asked.

"Yes ma'am." She said.

"Your total is $17.99" she said.

"Okay, how long?" I asked.

"Thirty minutes." She said and hung up.

I didn't have shit in my fridge so I made a mental note to get groceries one of these days I was free. I need to clean my house back the way I wanted it to look. Nothing was out of place, but I wanted to freshen it up.

Walking into my office I sat down and powered on my computer. Soon as it came on Princess' Picture popped up, the same picture I took of her when we went out on our second date.

Honestly, losing her is what made me want to leave the streets alone. I couldn't dare lose anyone else because of the shit I did. One thing about the streets is when you beef with someone they tend to fuck with your loved ones too just because they knew you was coming back for them to create more problems.

Searching on the internet I was looking for delicate buildings for sale and I ran across a few of them that I was interested in. I wanted something big, and the one that caught my attention was agreeable. It was a big two side-by-side building with nothing wrong with it. The inside was nice and roomy, and the outside was even better. I had things to get done, and I wanted shit happening before the month was over with.

Jasmine

"Ms. Knight." Yelled Ms. Clapper

"I'm paying attention." I said.

"No you're not, your falling asleep in class again." she said.

"I'm sorry." I said.

I was attending Grand Valley State University to become an RN and also working at Mercy Hospital as an assistant. I was now living in Muskegon Michigan, hoping for a better future. My classes were held in Grand Rapids still but I only went two days out the week which was Tuesdays and Thursdays.

I was working my ass off in school staying up late nights doing homework so I figured that had to be my reason for falling asleep in class so much, I just wanted to be finished so I could get my degree and move to another state. I was putting so much stress on myself,, I'm glad I don't look like what I've been through and what I'm going through because lord knows I would have been looking half dead.

"Ms. Knight I will be sending you an e-mail tonight." said Ms. Clapper. I didn't understand her attitude, it wasn't like I was behind in my work or failing, hell I just couldn't stay awake in her long ass sessions.

If my parents were alive to see how much I was causing myself to stress they would have been very upset with me. I had school loans to pay back, a car note, rent, utilities and I was doing a damn good job but sometimes it gets stressful doing things on my own but I guess it's life.

I really missed Kenny and I knew none of this would be happening if he was here but hey I guess shit happens and everything happens for a reason.

At first I didn't want to move from Grand Rapids but it was good that I did because I needed to focus more on me and the future that's ahead of me. Plus, I felt like my past was gone catch up with me so I needed to get away from everybody I dealt with back then. I didn't want to remember anything from my past and everything I left behind was sad memories and heartbreaks. Even though I attend school here I didn't socialize with nobody.

After the incident with Kenny and his side chick I haven't dated since then. I had guys dying for my attention but I had this bridge built and I wasn't letting my guards down for nobody, especially a nigga.

I knew it wasn't right for me to hold my past against everyone but I still felt like all dudes was the same and maybe I was wrong for blaming them for the hurt Kenny caused me but that was something I had to deal with.

I knew I deserved better, but I loved him so much that I couldn't allow him to enjoy life with the next bitch. I felt like I would have been a food to let another female take what I built, but they could have all that shit. All the trips to the clinics because of numerous STDS and the attack that caused me to have a miscarriage; I figured he would change but once he saw he had me sprung my feelings didn't faze him anymore. STUPID, was written across my forehead for still dealing with that man. Why did I allow him to treat me like that? Good thing I got smart and left him.

Class was done and it was time for me to head home, but listening to my growling stomach it said otherwise so I stopped at the cafeteria to order me something to eat.

"Hey Jasmine." said James.

"Hello James, how are you?" I asked.

"I'm good ma can't complain, you look good so need to ask you." He said.

"Looks can be deceiving." I said correcting him.

"Well I'm here whenever you want to talk." He said.

"Thanks." I said.

"Welcome." He said walking away.

If I didn't know any better I would say James stalked me. He was a cool ass person but nothing more than that. He had too many hoes at this college and even though I knew him way before they did I still wouldn't make him my man.

I received my food and headed back to the lobby. I didn't want to eat and drive so I decided to eat at the school. I ordered me a salad and a bottle of water. I loved my body, yes I ate fast food but I needed to make myself eat something healthier at least two days out the week.

My plans today was to go out on a shopping spree with Lia since we never get to do anything together for real. Her home wasn't too far from my school, so the ride wasn't going to be long at all.

I finished my food and headed to my car. I saw James and two girls standing across from my car and from the body language of one female you could tell they were arguing about something. He had so many girls, ain't no telling which one was his main.

Riding down the street I was enjoying the sunshine, I had my shades on and my sunroof open feeling like a million bucks. I was wearing my crème and black Chanel jumper with my wooden crème wedges.

Kenny didn't do nothing but make me stronger. He thought he brought me down but all he did was boost my ego and gave me the opportunity to love myself, which I should have been doing but it was true I loved Kenny more than I loved me, and that was the biggest mistake I ever made in life.

I pulled up to Lia house sitting in the car. I texted her and told her to bring her ass on. She was known for holding somebody up when it was time to go.

Lia was my hottie, her skin was still the lightest and she was a medium size chick who had no stomach, with thick thighs, curvy hips and shoulder length red hair. Lia was still attracted to those hood dudes who got MONEY, CARS, CLOTHES, AND comes with HOES. I was done with them, and didn't want anything to do with them.

"You cute hoe." I said.

"Thanks boo you looking good like always." she said. "Where are we going?"

"Let's tear the malls up and Detroit."

"Right up my alley boo." she said.

We were laughing and chit chatting about everything and enjoying each other's company. It's been a minute since I had a good laugh and not bullshit. Being with her I would always get a good laugh no matter what mood I was in.

"Remember that dude Rico?" She asked referring to one of her old freaks.

"Yeah, what about him?" I asked.

"Girl, he chicken nuggetttttt." We both laughed as she described the size of his tool.

"OMG. Really? And he was talking shit at the club like he had something down there." I said.

"You know how these niggas is and bitch you need to fuck before yo shit don't work no more." She laughed.

"Hoe don't do me, she still can get it wet and juicy." I said speaking for my pussy.

"That's hard to believe, when you gone get some dick?"

"When I feel like it, my toys do me just right. Also, I wasn't born with hands for nothing." I said. There was no need to lie, I been so horny lately to the point I get in the shower and let the water run down on my clit. It didn't feel like a human doing the job, but it was feeling pretty damn good to me. I promise you, the next time I have sex I'm gone walk around like I won a million dollars.

"Do you think he made it out?" She asked me.

"I'm not sure but let's not talk about that." I said. I really didn't know if Kenny was dead or alive, part of me cared and the other part didn't.

"How much longer that GPS say we got?" I asked changing the subject.

"Girl another hour. I'm taking me a nap." She said letting her seat back.

***

Pulling up to the Fairlane Town Center mall I had to do a face, and body check to make sure the wind didn't fuck anything up. Once my check-up was official we got out the car and made our way towards the entrance of the mall.

"Girl those are ugly." she yelled.

"You think so?" I asked.

"Hell yeah, you won't get no dick wearing those." She laughed causing the employees to laugh with her.

I loved Lia and her honesty, that's why I never kept a secret from her because she never judged me. Sometimes she could be too blunt, but deep down inside she's a sweet girl.

She wasn't a bad person she just did what she did. She never believed in sleeping with a man and not getting anything out of it. You wasn't gone leave her at home with a wet ass, you was giving her cash and hell people did it for free anyways so why not get some money. Some People would think she is a HOE because of what she did, but that wasn't her. She didn't sleep around with different kind of dudes, the dudes she messed with was the ones she'd been messing with for years.

Lia dealt with the wrong guys who turned her into a savage, but besides her crazy ways she was real sweet and had no problem helping anyone.

Heading out of the PINK store someone accidently bumped into me, not trying to cause any drama, I told them it was okay but of course Lia always had to be extra.

"Excuse you bitch." said Lia.

"What you just call me?" she asked.

"You heard me, I didn't stutter next time watch where you going." said Lia.

"Yeah whatever hoe," she said. Being with Lia people would think I was scary because she always jumped into something that involved me and someone else.

We had been in every store including the candy stores. Foot Locker was our last stop and this store was the one who always got more money from me because I was obsessed with tennis shoes and jogging suits.

"Jasmine?" Someone yelled as I turned around looking for faces.

"Kema? Hey." I said giving her a hug. "How you been?"

"Okay I guess." She said shrugging her shoulders.

Rushing our conversation like she had somewhere to go she kept looking over her shoulders as if she was hiding from someone. I followed her eyes, "naw that can't be" I said to myself. I knew I had to be tripping. Even though Kema could be ghetto and messy at times, she was still a beautiful girl.

"You ready boo?" Lia asked interrupting us.

"Yes, I'm getting tired girl."

"Something's iffy about that bitch and I can feel it."

"You just tripping, Kema's okay she just gossip too much." I said. Lia didn't like nobody ass but me, she always felt some kind of way about a female she saw me associating with.

After stopping at Sbarro's in the mall, we got us something to eat and were back on the road. Since I was tired and had been driving all-day I decided to let Lia drive so I can get me a nod in, but she wasn't buying it.

"Wake up and roll this dope up hoe." She yelled handing me a bag of weed and a blunt.

"Learn how to skip a day without smoking." We both laughed knowing that would never happen. Lia needed to smoke at least three times during the day, hell probably more than that. I hated the fact I learned how to roll because now Lia have me doing this shit for her 24/7.

"I got something to tell you boo." She said.

"What's up?" I asked.

"Listen. I was using the bathroom one specific day and my cat started to itch and burn when I started to pee, that's when the pain kicked in so I made a doctor's appointment and that's when I found out I had trichomoniasis."

"WHAT? OMG girl, do you know who gave it to you?" I asked as I jumped up in my seat.

"Bitch, it was Donte ugly ass. He's the only nigga I been fucking and I never thought about using protection with him since we've been messing around since our younger days." She admitted.

"Boo, you need to be careful. You know these niggas got dirty dicks. When did you find out?" I asked.

"Two days ago." She said.

"Oh my, everything gone be fine though, you know out of everybody I understand how you feel about it." Remembering how irritated and embarrassed I was when I found out several times Kenny had been cheating with multiple girls I should have left his ass then but I didn't. The feeling of having a disease is not good at all, I was so uncomfortable.

Finally, we pulled up to her house and I was worn-out from all the activities today such as work, school and going shopping with Lia. Being that I was free the next couple of days, my plans were to stay with Lia until she got tired of me.

"Bitch I'm going to get a drink." She said.

"I'm going in the house; I'll see you when you get back." I said getting out the car.

"When I get back you better be up and ready to turn up with your favorite girl." She said.

"Whatever." I said chucking up the deuces to her.

I walked inside the house making my way to her bedroom and jumped into her bed. The pressure from work and school was bringing me down but I had things to handle and I wouldn't do that by sitting on my fat ass. I didn't need to work the long hours I was working but I chose to so I could stay busy. I wasn't rich but I had enough money in the bank to get me by.

Once I got comfortable I picked up my kindle to finish up The Connects Wife by Nako. I didn't get far, but from what I read I knew it was going to be bomb as hell. Plus I heard so many people talking about this book. My favorite book which I read millions of times was Fallin For a Boss by Lucinda John. It's something about that damn Stacks that drives me crazy.

I rolled over to turn the T.V down but I didn't see the remote anywhere, and as I opened the dresser Lia nasty ass had everything in here. Condoms, pads, knives, mace and plenty of dildos. She was always known to be a freaky bitch.

Lia

Having my best friend in town was the best feeling ever. Living in two different cities changed our relationship a little. We didn't hang out or communicate like we use to, but I knew she was always one call away. Jasmine was the only person I trusted and the only person I had on my side. Our friendship meant everything to me. I considered her more than a friend she was the sister I never had and I'm sure the feelings were mutual.

Months after she lost her parents my nana died and that caused me to stress. I had lost a lot of weight and even my hair started to shed. I knew nothing about my biological parents but that was their lost, they missed out on raising a beautiful girl. . My nana never told me anything because she was afraid I would be hurt but little did she know I was already hurting inside not knowing who they were. I would never give up on my child no matter what the situation was.

Losing my nana and being with the wrong niggas fucked my attitude up. I was stuck up and wouldn't dare let a bum nigga touch me, even though I didn't need a nigga for shit. I dressed myself, bathed myself, slept with myself and sometimes use my fingers to fuck myself. I wasn't a basic bitch, and in my eyes there was no female who could compare to Lia Lee, I was my own competition.

I didn't wake up saying I wanted to be cold hearted, or I wanted to fuck this and that nigga. NO! Being down for the wrong person will introduce you to this lifestyle so I played niggas left to right.

To find out I had a disease broke me down, I was pissed, aggravated and ready to kill Donte hoe ass. I called and texted him several times and never got an answer back because he knew he had fucked up, but it was good because I was done with his trifling ass.

I pulled up to the corner store around the corner from my house, and once I got out the car I noticed Donte was coming out with another bitch. This explains why he stopped answering my calls, I knew he had to know he had that shit because he always answered my calls and I never ignored his calls when he wanted some pussy.

I felt stupid and ashamed of myself. Even though we weren't together we had an understanding. Unlike these other bitches they fuck a nigga and think his dick belongs to them. Me? I didn't give a fuck if you belong to Michelle Obama if we just fucking I will make sure feelings don't get involved and when you done carry yo ass back home with yo girl. You the one who got to lie to her not me so I have nothing to worry about.

I got out the car and marched my happy ass right over to his driver side window. His windows were tented so I couldn't see the expression on his face but I knew he was shocked to see me.

"You know you wrong right?" I asked, banging on the window.

"Man what you talking about?" he asked letting the window down.

"Maybe if you would have answered the phone you would know exactly what I'm talking about." I snapped.

"Donte who is this ghetto girl?" asked the female.

"Ghetto girl?" I snapped.

"Man chill," he said talking to the girl.

"No, who the fuck is she?" she snapped.

"Bitch who is you?" I yelled.

"I'm his wife who been with him for 4 years." she yelled.

"Wife? Well I'm his side bitch who been with him for three years, and by the way booboo you might want to get checked, because apparently I'm not the only one your husband been fucking," I snapped.

"Are you serious right now?" she yelled.

"Yes boo, very." I said as I walked off.

I couldn't believe this nigga was married, all this time he been lying saying he was single and only wanted me but I was playing games. I was hurt but more pissed off than anything because I always told myself I would never sleep with a married man, but now I could change that lie.

One thing I didn't understand was these niggas; they felt like they could mislead you while they got a bitch at home. To me a loyal bitch didn't mean shit to niggas now a days, because soon as they get one they dog her and treat her like shit hoping they can be forgiven. Even though we constantly forgave them at times we get tired of doing that shit when we know they'll never change.

Crazy part is, I been fucking this nigga for years and he's married. Only reason why I feel bad is because if I found out my husband was cheating on me I would be sad.

What be wrong with some females is they get dick happy and get to thinking he's there's when they already knew he had a girl, and then get to crying about some community dick. That's why I always say The worst thing is catching feelings for someone whose not yours, getting mad at everything they do forgetting it's not your place to feel that way. If you can't handle the shit then it's not made for you.

I got the drink and headed to my car, once I saw Donte was gone I drove off shaking my head. I couldn't wait to get back to my house and tell Jasmine what the hell just happened. Tonight I wanted to have one of our old fashioned girls night we'd normally have. I had so much on my mind and all I needed was to open up to her being she was the only person who understood me and never judged me.

Rolling down the street I put in my old mix C.D. and blasted Don't Trust No Nigga while I smoked my blunt, vibing to the music.

"You put yo trust in a nigga stupid hoe you figure

He won't fuck yo best friend and your sister

Ah lie to yah, and then screw yah and get mad if his homeboys do you

If he's a nigga don't let him fool yah

They all dogs that's what they do ah"

Pulling up to the house I couldn't wait to tell her the news that I just experienced with my own two eyes. I knew for a fact it was gone be shocking to her because it shocked the hell out of me as well. Hopping out the car I grabbed my things and ran to my front door.

Walking in the house I didn't see her so I knew her fat ass was in my bed sleeping. She better had hoped she didn't role into some nut. I'm playing I might be a crazy bitch but I'm not a nasty one.

"Bitch get the fuck up." I yelled jumping on my bed.

"Lia I'm tired man." She wined.

"We gotta turn up hoe." I said smacking her ass.

85

"Girl, guess the fuck what." I said sitting on the edge of the bed taking off my shoes.

"What?" she laughed.

"Donte was ignoring my calls, so I happen to run into him at the store and I noticed he had a female with him. Bitch I walked to his window and he was looking clueless when we rolled the window down. Come to find out he's been married for 4 years now, and when I told her to go get checked girl her eyes got bigger than my nipples" I laughed.

"Girl are you serious?" she asked.

"Yes bitch, I'm dead ass serious." I said still laughing.

"That shit wrong, I know she hurt." she said.

"Right, but that nigga would be dead if I was the wife." We both laughed as we got up to walk in the living room. Walking in the kitchen I grabbed some cups and ice and poured our drinks. Studying Jasmine facial expression I knew something was up with her.

"You good boo?" I asked.

"BITCH NOOO! I'M HORNY." She yelled.

My eyes got big because I wasn't expecting her to say something like that, hell I thought something important was really bothering her.

"Omg, are you serious?" I laughed.

"Yes hoe." She chuckled back.

"Well I don't have a dick." I laughed pointing in between my legs.

"Girl gone, you're silly." She said.

We were definitely feeling ourselves because we got up and danced around the living room like we was at the club. Every time we got together we always showed our asses, not caring what anybody had to say about us. We both done been through a lot in life, but one thing we did was made sure we got back on our shit.

"I love you sis." She said

"I love you more, bitch we drunk. "I laughed twerking in my chair.   "I need to fuck." She said.

"I know you do hoe, it's been too long." I laughed.

"Girl, when somebody get up in this I'm telling you I'm gone act an ass on him." She said riding the arm of my couch.

***

The next morning Jasmine woke me up with some breakfast. She had fixed a sista some cheesy eggs, bacon, pancakes, grits, fresh strawberries and can't forget the O.J.

"Thanks sis." I said appreciating her cooking for me.

"You welcome girl I got a hangover so I knew you was gone be hungry." she said.

"Hell yeah and this shit good." I said digging in my plate like a dog.

Finishing up the food I made sure I helped her clean up the mess we made because we definitely fucked up the living room last night. I got up brushed my teeth and took my medicine. I had to make sure I was taking my meds right so I could get rid of this fast and not slow.

Getting ready for work I jumped into my blue scrubs. I was working part time as an assistant at Saint Mary's Hospital.

Today was supposed to be one of my off days but my boss asked me if I could come in and cover a 4 hour shift and I said yes because it was easy money.

I used to work at the Strip Club and that's what made my bank account fat like it is. There was never a dry night, I made money every day. The least I made was $3,000 a night shaking my ass, popping and twisting was the lifestyle I lived back then until one specific night, which made me give up the stripping life.

I was walking out the door on my way home. I was tired, my ass cheeks were sore and I needed to go home take a bath and just relax. Tonight I made a lot; I never counted my money until I got home. I knew it was a lot, I never had any doubt about that.

Walking to my car I kept hearing footsteps behind me but I didn't see anything every time I turned around. Once I opened the car door a hand quickly was wrapped around my face. I was shocked and couldn't move.

"What do you want with me?" I cried.

He didn't say anything, he threw me in the back of a van and tried pulling my pants down but I was kicking and yelling the whole time. Once he heard voices, he grabbed me by the back of my neck and threw me on the ground.

I jumped up and ran back to my car and he pulled off. Three people came over running asking was I ok and if I needed them to call the police. I didn't want the police involved so I left it at that and got in the car and pulled off.

After that I told myself I'll never shake my ass on a pole again. Standing in the kitchen with Jas I was on my way out the door for work.

"Tonight we are turning up hoe, as in going out." Reminding her that she wouldn't be sitting in the house another night. I wanted her to get out and enjoy her life before she's a little old lady.

"That's fine let's turn up in yo city." She danced around the kitchen.

"That's cool. See you when I get out hoe." I kissed her cheek and left.

I pulled up into work and sat in my car for about ten minutes. I still couldn't believe this nigga gave me a disease and if his bitch wanted problems we could have them. I haven't mopped the floor with a bitch in a long time and she was gone be my next victim if she came for me.

Walking through the entrance of the hospital I noticed Donte wife was walking out crying. I looked at her and she looked back at me.

"You got it too?" I laughed.

"Fuck you bitch." She said.

"Yo man did enough of that." I laughed and walked off.

I didn't know her reasons for being here but from the looks of her tears it was something serious. I probably was wrong for what I said but oh well shit happens. Putting my belongings in my locker inside the breakroom I heard my phone go off. Once I saw who it was it took away the happiness I came into work with.

Donte- man I apologize for what happened. I wasn't fucking nobody but you and my wife and comes to find out she was the one cheating and gave it to me so that's how you had to get it. I really am sorry. Me and her not together anymore.

I didn't even text him back, but damn, how the hell he gone leave her because she was cheating? And he was cheating with me? See, niggas be having life all fucked up and get mad when we do the shit to them that they do to us. I'm not saying it's okay for bitches to cheat and think like a nigga, but now a days you have no choice so you wouldn't get played like a bitch.

Hearing some yelling coming from the back room I overheard some co-workers arguing and being the nosey person that I was I walked straight to the back room and got front row seat.

"That's just my baby daddy, he up for grabs bitch I don't want his broke ass." Said one female. I was cracking the fuck up because they were in there talking a lot of shit about a nigga. But that's one thing I hate about females too, they meet a nigga and find out he broke as hell but still end up having sex with him and soon as she get pregnant and he leave her ass she want to start calling him broke.

"He must ain't too broke you laid down with him." Said the other one.

"Fuck you." Said the first one feeling like shit.

Soon as they started heading for each other the security guards pulled them back from each other to keep down any confusion. Walking down the hallway I decided to call Jasmine to make sure she didn't change her mind on me about going out, since she tends to do that a lot.

"Yes boo?" she answered the phone.

"Did you still wanna go out tonight?" I asked.

"Yes girl, you sure you can do it?" she asked.

"Hell yea, I can show you better than I can tell you." I said.

"Okay, turn up then." She said.

"Okay, that's cool." I said.

I had exactly 45 minutes left until it was time for my shift to end, which left us three hours to get ready. Even though we knew we was already gone be late you could never rush perfection.

***

"Girl I hope I can find something." Jas said getting into the car. One thing about shopping at the last minute, you had to rush and put something cute together.

"Yeah me too." I said, inhaling this bomb ass weed that I copped from my homeboy. He was the only one who supplied me good. I always smoked that White Rhino, which did me just right and had me on cloud 20.

"Tell me why I saw Donte wife leaving the hospital today and you know I had to say something to her." I laughed.

"Bitch what you say?"

"You got it too? And she told me fuck me and I said yo man did that enough." I said. We both laughed and Jas found that shit too funny.

"You hell man, I can't stand you." She laughed even harder because she knew I wasn't wrapped too tight. I think my nana dropped me on my head when I was a baby, because I was missing hella screws.

Riding down Eastern, it was a typical Friday, 82 degrees outside so you know all the thots was coming out tonight, probably out selling their food stamps just to get there hair done and to buy them an outfit, and can't forget about the granny's who had to miss out on Friday night bingo because they had to babysit their bad ass grandbabies. Some of these mothers were pathetic if you ask me.

"Bitch turn this up, I don't care how old it is this is my shit." she said dancing to No Love by Scrappy.

Soon as we made it to the mall I parked the car and we walked inside. Tonight the mall was packed and everybody was running around looking for last minute shit. When it came to partying in Grand Rapids you was capable of having a good time. They showed love and made you feel welcome. It was a few bitches who hated, but that was everywhere you went.

"Here you ladies go. Tonight my homeboy having his grand opening at his club and you sexy ladies should come through. I'm telling you ma, it's gone be worth it and me and my niggas would certainly show you a good time. In fact, since y'all looking fine as fuck I'll make sure yall get into the V.I.P section for free." He said handing us some flyers.

"We will make sure we come." I said winking my eye at him. This nigga was fine as fuck. His gear was up to date; he was a caramel skin nigga with some hazel eyes. He wore his low fade to perfection and I couldn't wait to shake my ass on him.

Purchasing our items we paid our tabs and hurried out the mall. Once we got in the car I damn near did 50 out the parking lot. I had to stop and grab a bottle for our pre-turn up while we got ready at the house.

"Run in and run out." She said.

"I am, that's why I'm keeping the car running."

I grabbed us a bottle of Remy Martin and headed out the corner store.

"Aye ma, slow down." One of the corner boys said dying for my attention.

"You don't want me nigga I got six kids at home." I lied. I couldn't take half the shit I said at times myself. I was a goof ball and wasn't no way around it.

"I 'don't mind playing step daddy." He yelled as I got in the car. I laughed for a minute and closed the door before he got another word out his mouth.

"I'm ready to have fun." She said.

"Hopefully yo lonely ass meets a man." I said. I knew Jasmines ass was horny as fuck. She didn't even let a nigga get a taste of her juice box. Even though I wouldn't want to just fuck on anything I wouldn't mind a nigga slurping me up.

"Fuck you hoe." She said rolling her eyes.

We got to the house and my ass basically jumped out the car trying to get inside. I don't know why we were rushing; it isn't like black people do shit on time anyway. There's not one black person I know who isn't slow when it came to getting ready for an event.

"I'm going to shower." I said leaving her in the living room.

"I am too that's why I'm glad you got two bathrooms."

Standing in the shower I made sure I washed up multiple times. One thing my nana didn't play about was a female and her body. She always made sure me and Jasmine kept our selves clean.

Peeking out the shower my phone rung displaying Donte's name on the front of the screen. There was nothing for us to talk about and I really didn't feel like hearing his lying ass stories but I answered anyway.

"What man?" I said. I already knew he was trying to get in good with me but that was never going to happen. I had some feelings for Donte but he fucked that up and I'm not falling for that shit with his wife. Donte was a hoe so I know we weren't the only ones he was having sex with. He ate my ass on the first night I met him.

"So you really done fucking with a nigga?" He yelled through the phone sounding as if he didn't get the picture I was trying to draw.

"Fuck youuuu I'm good on yo ass dawg." I said.

"You fucking somebody else?" he asked.

"What I do isn't your concern." I said and hung up.

I wasn't having sex with him anymore especially since I was almost done clearing up what he had given me the first time. Even though he had some good dick I wasn't putting myself in that situation again. Dick was good but not that good to keep putting your life in danger.

Once I got out the shower I wrapped up in my towel and ran into my room to finish getting ready. I dried off quickly and put some lotion on.

Since the weather wasn't too bad out I decided to wear my hot pink tight fitted club dress that hugged every curve I had. The dress had my back out and my sleeves were short.. On my feet were my all-white Prada heels that were still brand new, fresh out the box. To complete my outfit I had on my white and pink bracelets with the earring to match.

Standing at the mirror fixing my hair, Jas walked out the bathroom in her fit and my best friend was killing shit. I knew I had the baddest bitch on my arm with no doubt about that.

Jasmine wore an all-black tight fitted dress. One sleeve was long and the other was short, with part of her chest showing. Her black red bottoms, and red lipstick is what popped out. Her jewelry was red and silver to match her purse.

"Beautiful." I said staring her up and down.

"Thanks ma." she said.

I walked into the kitchen to pour us some drinks that would get us started for the night.

"Here you go bitch we need to get a buzz or something." I laughed handing her a cup of Remy.

"You right about that." She said gulping down here drink. After we finished our drink we took at least four more shots to get us started.

Walking in the living room I stood by the mirror that hung on my wall admiring myself before I left out the door. I was a sexy ass chick that niggas referred to as a "Red Bone". My red hair is what drove niggas crazy and the pussy is the shit that kills them. I knew I was taking home some numbers tonight.

I was told by millions of people that I put you in the mind of the singer Ciara, but much thicker in the hips and thighs. I was tall as shit and still had a bad ass shape to go with it. We got in Jas' car and headed to the club. I pulled out my blunt from my purse that I rolled back at the house.

"Bitch turn that up." I said snapping my fingers to the beat. She was blasting Real Sisters by Future.

Say you getting throwed, I'm tryna pour up with you

Oh that's your best friend, I'm tryna fuck her with you

First met the bitch, they said they real sisters

I don't give a fuck if they was real sisters

Fuck around with me, you tryna dodge bullets

Serving packs of chickens in a dodge hemi

Fuck around with me, you tryna dodge bullets

Fuck around with me, I fuck twin sisters

It was 10:45 p.m. and we were just now pulling up to the club, both getting out the car looking sexy as ever. Once she locked the car up we made our way to the entrance. The line was wrapped around the corner and I didn't feel like standing here.

"Aye ma, come over here." Someone yelled.

Once I followed the voice I saw it was the dude earlier from the mall who handed us those flyers. He had on some all-red Robin Jeans with a regular black V-neck tee and some black Jordan's. The chain that danced around his neck almost blinded my ass from all the diamonds.

Walking inside the club all eyes was on us. We had niggas and bitches breaking necks. Even though we haven't been out in a while attention was something we were used to. Forgetting about all the drama we had going on, we just wanted to have a good time.

Making our way to the V.I.P. section we saw all kinds of drinks sitting on the table inside a big blue bowl. There was Remy Martin, Grey Goose, Cîroc, Alize and some Hennessey. With the weed in my system I was already high as a kite.

"So what are your names?" He asked us as he took a seat next to us.

"I'm Lia and that's my sister Jasmine." I said introducing us. He kept licking his lips at me not knowing he was drowning my thong. "We didn't get your name."

"My name Moe lil mama but aye check this out, I gotta make a run and I'll be back to check on y'all. Enjoy ya selves and behave." He smiled showing off his brilliant smile.

"Damn he looking good standing right there." said Jasmine. I followed her eyes and noticed some dark skin dread head nigga was looking in our way.

"Yeah he is cute." I said.

Dancing to the beat of Mila J- My Main we noticed some females on the dance floor thought they was killing shit but they wasn't doing nothing. They skinny asses had no ass or thighs.

"Come on bestie let's shut this shit down like old times." I said as we got up making our way to the dance floor.

One of the baddest chicks in this club, dat my main

One of the only girls that I love, dat my main

Been down with her since day one, dat my main

Can't nobody break this up, dat my main

We'll never fight over them boys, dat my main

We be playing with these dudes like toys, dat my main

Once we did our thing, the chicks looked at us and went back to their seats. We were still on the dance floor fucking shit up. Since I used to be a certified stripper, I knew all the right dances to make some dicks hard.

"Fuck it up then bestie." Said Jas. All the attention was on us and we were giving them the show they wanted to see.

Soon as the song went off the DJ slowed the party down and I was glad because I didn't want to sweat my hair out.

Grinding to Pornstar by August Alsina. The crowd was getting excited to see us rolling our bodies to every beat of the song. Jasmine kept catching sexy chocolate watching her so then she really gave him a show since he wanted to play peekaboo.

To see the excitement on my girl face made me happy, because I can't remember the last time I actually saw her smile this much.

I was too busy grinding my ass on some random dude and didn't even notice Jasmine had disappeared, I guess the dance was worth it. As I looked around for Jasmine I finally found her at the V.I.P. section drinking shots back to back.

"Thanks for the dance." I said as I made my way over to my girl.

"Don't leave me like that again you had me worried." I snapped at her.

"My bad bitch, calm the fuck down." She shot back. We laughed and had us some more drinks. I was tired from shaking my ass so now I wanted to kick back and relax.

"How you doing Ms. Lady"? Sexy chocolate finally decided to approach Jasmine.

"I'm doing good and you sir? Jasmine nervously replied.

"You looking good but I'm living can't complain." he said back to her. He wasn't no ugly guy both his swag was something exclusive and his hair was neatly dreaded.

From the looks of it they wanted to enjoy their conversation more so I got up and walked off giving them some privacy. Making my way to the dance floor I came across the dude I was dancing with before I walked off to find Jasmine.

"Oh now you wanna join me ma?" he asked.

"Honey I can leave." I said. Sizing him up my eyes danced all around him figuring out the kind of person he was by looking at his attire. Attached to his ass he had on a pair of bleached Robin Jeans with a Versace pullover with his timberland boots. "Thug" I said to myself as I finished looking him up and down.

"Calm down boo you could stay I was just playing."

"What's your name ma?" he asked me, licking those juicy ass lips.

"Lia and what's yours Mr.?" I flirted back.

"My name Twan boo." He said.

"Oh I'm your boo now?" I laughed.

"You can be whatever you want to be." He said as he rubbed his fingers across my face.

"Is that right? You sure yo bitch won't be mad?" I asked making sure he was single.

"Damn, if I did have one why she gotta be all that? But for your information I'm single. I wouldn't even be here if I was tied down." He responded back letting me know he was available.

"I like to hear that." I said.

"Where yo nigga at? The one you were grinding on earlier." He asked sounding jealous.

"Oh so now you stalking me? If you must know that wasn't my nigga I was just having a good time." I snapped back realizing I was explaining myself to a nigga who wasn't mine.

As our conversation got good, I looked towards the bar and noticed Donte was over that way. I knew right then it was my cue to leave. I didn't have time to fight and argue with him so I avoided all of that and decided I should go home.

"You good ma?" he asked me.

"Yeah I gotta go find my sister I'm getting tired." I lied trying to escape.

"Can I get your number?" he asked me. I took his phone from him, programmed my number and made my way over to Jasmine and sexy chocolate.

"I'm sorry sexy chocolate it's time for me and my girl to go." I said removing her from her male friend she had met.

"I enjoyed your company baby girl, make it home safe." He said as he kissed her hand. Making our way through the club I told Jasmine the reason I was ready to leave and she laughed like the shit was funny.

"Girl I don't want him to see me." I said.

"Just keep walking, it's crowded he won't even notice it was you." She said. The club was getting ready to close anyway so I don't know why he's just getting here, unless he was already here and we didn't notice one another.

"So did you get his number?" I asked, soon as we got inside the car.

"You know I did girl." she slurred between her words, looks like she had one to many drinks.

"That's what I'm talking about you gone use it?" I asked, knowing her all she was gone do is let it go to waste.

"Yes, sure is." She said smiling.

Luckily we made it home safe, pulling up to the house my phone started to ring from a number I didn't even know.

"Hello?" I answered.

"Did you make it home?" asked the male.

"First I didn't know who you were, but now that I recognize your voice yes I made it thanks for checking." I said.

"Dang, you got niggas calling your phone like that." he joked but low key I knew he was serious. But little did he know lil Lia didn't play.

"No, don't even play me." I laughed through the phone.

"I'm just fucking with you baby girl." Said Twan.

"Ok. Cool, hit me up tomorrow." I said making the conversation short. I was feeling myself too much and I didn't have time to talk on the phone.

"Sure will, goodnight." he said.

"Night." I said.

Walking inside the house I slung my keys and purse across the living room table and Jas did the same thing. We were drunk and didn't have any energy.

"Bestie I had fun." She said. I can tell by the tone of her voice she was slumped.

"Me too glad you got out tonight." I responded back to her.

Making our way to the room we both took off our clothes with the little energy we had left. I wrapped my hair up and got in the bed with my bestie. We weren't gay, but every chick got that one specific friend they do shit like this with.

Not even twenty minutes had passed and Jasmine was already snoring in my damn ear so it wasn't any reason to tell her drunk ass goodnight.

Thinking about everything I had recently went through with Donte, never again will I sleep without protection, even if we been together for five years I wasn't going out like that. Damn! I was going to miss Donte big dick ass, but I had to leave him the fuck alone. The new dude I had met tonight had my nose wide open and I didn't even know him like that. He was smooth and laid back. His conversation was real good and I enjoyed every minute of it. I had a huge thing for those caramel skin dudes. It was something about them that I loved.

Nights like this I hated to be lonely, I needed some attention between my legs and I needed it bad. I wanted to call Donte but I just couldn't do that to myself. His actions proved he did not give a fuck about me so I had to stop giving a fuck about him.

The night was winding down and I was drunk and tired needing to carry my ass to sleep. I took out my phone and snapped a picture of Jasmine. She was out of it and I couldn't wait to show her this picture. Before I closed my eyes I said my prayers and kissed the picture of my nana that sat on my night stand. Lord knows I missed her so much.

Jasmine

My head was banging, my mouth was dry and my stomach was hurting. I had a bad hangover but I could say last night was well needed and I enjoyed every minute of it.

I wasn't an alcoholic but once it's time to have fun, liquor wasn't a stranger to me. I knew how to hold my liquor and still be a lady at the same time.

"Lia I'm finna leave." I said shaking her.

"Why? Stay with me some more." She whined with slob on her face, barely keeping her eyes open.

"I'll be back or you can come down there." I went in the bathroom and handled my morning breath. I couldn't stand a funky breath person, the shit was all bad.

Looking down at my phone I was receiving a call from someone who wasn't stored but I answered it anyway.

"Wassup baby girl?" A deep voice greeted me as soon as I answered it.

With a smile on my face I said back. "Hey, what's going on?" For some reason I remembered his voice like it's been around me for years.

"Sorry if I woke you I was trying to see if you made it home safely cause I see you and your home girl was turnt up too much." he laughed.

"Yeah, I did I'm hitting the highway on my way home now as we speak." I said.

"Oh? You don't live here in Grand Rapids?" he asked.

"Nope. I was visiting my home girl I live in Muskegon. Is this your city? I said.

"Small world I live in Muskegon too I never seen you around." He said.

"That's a good thing right?" I asked.

"Yeah, that's good, what you got up for today?" He asked.

"Nothing probably just gone chill for the day." I said.

"On a Saturday? Girl you better get out and enjoy this nice weather." He giggled through the phone.

"I might, I have homework that needs to be done." I said back.

"Is that right? I love a smart chick ma. Maybe we can get out later on or something?" he said.

"That would be cool. I would love that."

"Drive safe and I'll give you a call once I think you made it home." we said our goodbyes and then hung up.

Even if I wanted to lie I couldn't. I wanted him more than he wanted me. His dark skin was smooth, and the way he talked made my juices flow. I never had someone make me wet by the tone of their voice until I met superman. The thought of meeting someone felt good inside but I didn't want to take things further than us being friends. Afraid of what I've been through before I just wanted things to stay calm for now.

Snapping me out my thoughts I heard Lia ringtone playing on my phone letting me know her crazy ass was calling me.

"Girl what yo hot ass do last night while I was sleep? I answered the phone.

"Nothing girl, I went to bed too but my boo did call me and check on me, girl you was knocked out." She said.

"You better had not been fucking while I was in the bed with you." I laughed.

"Now you know I wouldn't do that." she said.

"Better not have but girl hold on someone's beeping through my line." I said.

I looked at the phone and it was my superman calling me back I must have been on his mind heavy because he was on mine knocking my brain out.

"Hello?" I answered the phone.

"You made it here yet?" he asked.

"Almost." I said.

"You got anything planned once you touch down?" he asked.

"Nope I don't. What's up?"

"Breakfast at Denny's?"

"Sure, I'll text you the address." I said.

Lia had hung up on the other line so I said forget it, I'll just call her back after my date. Hearing No Love on the radio the other day made me want to play it all over again and this time I could put it on repeat since I had the old C.D.

I'm so tired of going up and down round in round

I'm so over it, I'm breaking down, I'm bout to call it quits

I then had enough of it, my heart is so cold I can't find no love here

Finally, I pulled up to my house and my feet were sore but I didn't want to miss this date for nothing. All that dancing we did last night was now paying me back and I was sure to soak in the tub when I returned back home.

When I got to the front door I noticed a piece of paper on the steps that said "YOU SHOULD HAVE FINSIDHED WHAT YOU STARTED" In red marker. My heart almost jumped out in front of me because someone is watching me. Didn't nobody know where I lived but Lia, well at least that's what I thought?

Is he alive? Is this someone playing jokes with me? Millions of questions were going through my head and the first person that came to mind was Kenny. If this was him I knew he wouldn't go to the police with this because all he wanted to do was get back at me. If he wanted to go to war with a bitch I was ready for it all.

I ran inside the house and looked in the mirror to make sure I was half decent cause hangovers would have you looking like you been in a cat fight with someone. Running inside the bathroom I took a quick shower to make sure my body was fresh, and then I ran in the room and slipped on some clothes. I wanted to look fresh for my first date since Kenny. Since I found this note on my door steps I was dying to get out of here, I was scared as hell. I had nobody here to protect me or make me feel safe. I made a mental note to bring some knives into my bedroom with me before I go to sleep.

Standing in the living room I heard loud music coming from outside, so I peeked out the window and noticed he was coming to the door.

He pulled up in a black Escalade. He was looking good like he was going back to the club or something but all he wanted was to go to breakfast. I was wearing a tight fitted PINK jump suit from Victoria's Secret and some Chanel flip flops. My hair didn't sweat out too bad so I threw it into a messy bun and added some MAC lip gloss.

"Good morning beautiful." He said standing there looking like a darker Waka Flocka.

"Good morning handsome." I said. This man was so darn sexy to me that I couldn't help but think of naughty things.

He opened the door for me and helped me get into his truck. Once he got in his Gucci cologne filled my nostrils. A man that dressed nice and smelled even better was a plus. I hated the fact that his smell had me thinking about Kenny, just because it was the same cologne being used. Ugh!

"You even look good in active wear, do you work out sometimes?" he asked breaking the silence.

"Thanks, you look good too but aren't you over dressed just to be going to breakfast and yes sometimes me Lia might go work out, the one that calls you sexy chocolate." We both laughed.

"Thanks Ma, this just an everyday thing for me." He said.

We pulled up to Denny's that wasn't too far from my apartment, looking at the parking lot it wasn't too many cars and I was glad.

Slim helped me out the car and we walked in holding hands like teenagers. We both sat down and ordered our food, but I was kind of skeptical about what I should get because I didn't know how his pockets looked. Denny's wasn't expensive so I'm guessing he had more than enough.

"So baby girl tell me something about you." he said licking those lips.

"Well I'm a nurse assistant at Mercy Health Hospital, attending college still, I have no kids, I love shopping and taking care of business, if I'm not working or in school I just sit in the house and read. I'm the only child I have no family here it's just me. What do you do?" I replied with confidence when I mentioned my career.

"That's good, I like that. I graduated from high school and college and received my degree in business. Matter of fact, the club you and your home girl visited was mine and next door to that is where I got my restaurant going, also I just opened up a teen youth center." He replied rubbing his chin hairs.

From his appearance I would have thought he was a drug dealer, but when he mentioned having his degree and all that made me wetter below. A black man with goals is something that's hard to come by and I was in love already. When I first saw him I just knew he was another Kenny.

It was something about Slim that was driving me crazy and truth be told I wanted to jump across the table landing straight on his lap without any clothes, but I kept telling myself that I needed to take control of my sexual feelings. But that was hard as hell when I felt like a virgin again.

"Ma? You with me? Is that enough information for you?" he laughed as he broke the lustful thought I had in my head.

"Yes that's enough information for me." I finally said in embarrassment.

We were definitely feeling each other; well at least I know I was. I was trying my best to not act nervous around him but fuck it I couldn't help it. He kept smiling and staring at me with those dark brown eyes he had. The vibe around us was good and that's how I wanted it to stay.

We ate our food and he left a three hundred dollar tip. I had a nice date with him and I was looking forward to plenty more.

Pulling back up to my place we sat here long enough to get a couple of laughs from each other.

"I enjoyed breakfast." I nervously said.

"So did I baby girl. I wanna do it again sometime." He said. I agreed that we can go out another time, hell I wanted to enjoy the rest of my day with him.

I got out the car and headed to my front door. I made my ass jiggle in my jogging suit just to give him something to stare at; I knew he was already looking because every man on this earth looked at a female's ass.

I couldn't believe I had a chance to go out with this handsome man. He was intelligent and I could tell by the way he spoke on relationships that he's experienced heartbreak. It's life, something we all have to experience heartbreak but then we have to decide if it's worth it or not.

Walking inside my house I pulled my gun out my purse just in case something wasn't right. I didn't have a bad feeling or anything but you should always be prepared when you have a bad past.

Heading into the bathroom I ran me some bath water and made sure it was nice and hot. The way my body felt I needed this hot water to heal and attack all the aches and pain that were created last night.

Sitting in the water I called Lia to tell her about my breakfast date. I knew she was gone have a million questions so I was prepared.

"Hello?" she answered sounding like she was asleep.

"Wake your ass up." I said.

"Girl, I'm so tired." She said.

"Me too, but anyway I went out to breakfast with sexy chocolate." I said sounding like a high school girl who just had their very first date.

"Oot. I'm awake now. How was it?" she yelled, sounding like she had jumped out the bed.

"It was nice, he's cool. The club we went to was his and he also has a restaurant next door to it." I said.

"About time you meet somebody with some sense." She laughed.

"You got your nerves all those thugs you be dealing with." We both shared a laugh because she knew I wasn't lying.

"You had your share so please don't forget. I'm excited for you though boo."

"Yeah you're right about that. Well, I was just calling you to tell you about my date, I need to catch up on some sleep." I said. Once we said our goodbyes the call was disconnected.

Letting my body soak in the tub I laid my head back and relaxed. Today and tomorrow I just wanted it to be a chill day for me until I go back to work and school. I had homework to catch up on and a test to study for so that was gone keep me busy.

Washing my body, I made sure I washed everything at least six times. Rinsing the suds off me I got out and wrapped my towel around me. Looking in the bathroom mirror I was staring at a brilliant woman. I was strong, hardworking and beautiful. I refuse to give up. I'm focused, handles my business well but all I wanted was someone to see what I saw.

I always wanted someone to be proud of me, but I had no one. I knew if my parents were alive they'd be happy for their baby girl. Making a mental note I wanted to stop by and visit their grave and add some more flowers.

I made my way to my bedroom and dried off; I didn't even feel like getting dressed so I jumped into bed naked. Once I got comfortable my phone beeped, indicating that someone was texting me.

Slim: I wish you well with your test day after tomorrow. Good luck and get some rest because I know you're tired from last night. Lol

Me: thank you handsome, I'm resting now. Just bathed and now I'm laying here with nothing on.

Slim: mhhm, don't tease me ma.

I smiled and said my prayers closing my eyes letting sleep get the best of me.

Slim

I woke up this morning with nobody but Jasmine on my mind. I couldn't lie, I was feeling shorty but I didn't want to seem desperate. If this was God giving me a second chance at love there was nothing I was gone do to fuck up.

She was independent and that's what I loved most about her. Her attitude made me want her more. She was beautiful to me in all kind of ways. I wanted her, I got her and I wasn't letting her go. With all her flaws and non-perfect past I was still willing to have her apart of my future.

Despite my past situation I couldn't believe I was falling for someone else. I thought I'll never end up in this situation again from the last time I was dealing with Princess, as much as I tried to not allow myself to catch feelings for Jasmine it was too damn late because shorty had me gone. Even though we had just met each other, being around her for that short period of time I felt something that I hadn't felt in a long time, love, that deep intense feeling. When we first met, I knew it was something just by the way we clicked and I never clicked with any chick that easily. For a minute, I thought it was that liquor talk, but the more I thought about her the more I knew it was real.

Getting back to the basics, in the past weeks I spent in Grand Rapids I ended up investing into two big buildings that sat side by side which I knew would be the location for my restaurant and club. I spent cash money for it but it didn't faze me because I deserved it. I ended up naming them both "Blue Horizon". This was just a simple name that I came up with because blue was my favorite color but other than that there was no reason behind it.

I hired strippers and waitress for the club and some big niggas for security guards. The ladies wore some all-white high wasted shorts with a crop top blue shirt with the club logo printed across the shirt on their breast.

Everything was officially going good with the youth center also. The location of that was in Muskegon. I found a couple of teens who wanted to be here from time to time, and my door was open for anyone else who needed me. I was hoping to expand my restaurant in more cities, big cities at that. All I needed to do was buy more buildings elsewhere and that's what I planned on doing with all the free time I had on my hands. This was perfect for me, something that would keep me out of trouble.

Rock was rocking with me no matter what, he even helped me out at the club. Moe was helping but not too much. He said a few slick comments under his breath but I didn't let that shit faze me. I never thought I was too good to be in the hood or catching plays but sometimes that shit got out of control and hot. I would never forget where I came from but I'm gone always remember where I'm trying to go and that was not back to prison or the graveyard.

I had goals that I wanted to accomplish before I leave this earth and being around fuck niggas daily wasn't gone get me nowhere but back in trouble.

Walking around my house I admired the work and decorations my mom added to my place. She said my house was too plain for her, but I was a guy and I'm sure people understood. I didn't need all that fancy shit as long as I had a roof over my head I was more than straight.

My living room was decorated in smoke gray and red. I had a gray sectional with grey and black checker pillows on it. My table was black with the red cushions on the chairs and pictures hung on the wall of my family. My room was all-black with a big black area rug under my bed and some pictures of me and my sister.

Stepping in the bathroom I turned the water on from the shower, got in and let the hot water run down my back. I needed to get back in the gym because I felt like I was losing my strength and that was a big problem.

Going down memory lane this hot water caused me to think about the day my lil sister had got killed.

"Hey baby sis." I said walking in the house.

"Hey big brother." She said.

"Why you sitting out here alone?" I asked her.

"No reason, ain't nothing to do really, my friends gone with their boyfriends." She said.

"Yeah, you know I 'on play that shit." I said.

I walked inside the house and greeted my mom and dad sitting in the living room watching some T.V.

"Hey son, what's up?" said my dad.

"What's good pops and nothing much, same thing." I said.

"I understand." He said.

I walked into my room, and as soon as I started to count my money all I heard was gun shots outside and people screaming.

I ran down stairs and saw some niggas shooting in front of my house, and I yelled and told my mom and dad to lie down and soon as I got outside one of the niggas was standing in the street shooting directly towards my living room window causing the glass to brake.

POW! POW! POW!

I shot back, and they jumped in the car and drove off leaving my sister on the ground with six gun shots wounds in her chest.

"MAAAAAAAA! Get up baby." I said.

"Oh lord, nooooooo." Yelled my mom.

"Call 911please." Said my dad.

All I could do was hold my sister in my arms, crying and shaking. Laying before me was her dead body and she had nothing to do with this.

"It's your fault." Said my dad.

"How? I don't know who they were." I cried.

He start coming towards me swinging, and at this moment I didn't care about him hitting me because I felt I deserved it. I was supposed to protect them and make sure that nobody came looking for me, but I didn't.

The tears streaming down my face caused me to snap out of my thoughts. I didn't want my sister thinking I forgot about her when I didn't.

Jumping out the shower I dried off and walked into my room. Searching in my dresser for some boxers I ran across a picture of princess. The fucked up thing about it is I had no signs or evidence leading me to the person who did this. For all I know I could be walking by them every day and wouldn't know it was them who did it.

Sitting in the visiting room staring at all the families laugh, cry, and joke around made me think about my mom. I didn't like her to come down here and see me caged up like an animal, a letter and talking on the phone was good enough for me. When I finally looked up at the door I saw something so beautiful walking in and it gave me chills and made me smile.

"Hey king." She said.

"Sup boo." I said.

"So, what's up?" she said meaning if I heard anything about my time in here yet.

"I ain't sure right now, but you know I 'on won't you out here stressing over me, gone head live life and do you." I said.

She didn't say anything; she just sat there looking at me with hurt in her eyes.

"I'm just saying; if you ever feel lonely do you. All I ask for is some letters, and to accept my calls and we good boo." I said.

"I hear you." She said with tears in her eyes.

"Don't cry ma, we gone be good. I'm gone be good, whatever they throw at a nigga you know I can handle it. I'm Slim baby." I said.

"I love you man, this so hard." She said.

"Keep yo head up, this life and I knew the consequences." I said.

We talked about old times, laughed around for a minute then the guard came and told us we had five minutes left for visitation. Something was strange about her because I was the one who did all the talking; she barely looked a nigga in the eyes. I wasn't ready for her to leave, but I know there will be another time.

"Ride or die baby." She said.

"Bet ma, like I told you, do you and don't settle for less, you deserve the world baby, don't let no pussy nigga fuck over you." I said.

Slipping on my Nike sweats, white tank top with my all white Air force ones I was heading out to Wal-Mart to pick up a few groceries for my house. Cooking was one of my specialties besides sex; I could cook my ass off. I wasn't like other niggas around here, I grocery shopped the right way. I wasn't into all those Hungry Man dinners; I needed the works, those old fashioned soul-food meals my grandma and mother use to cook growing up.

Walking out the door I noticed an all-white Dodge Dart was parked in front of my house. As I got a little closer I couldn't see who was inside because of the dark tents that covered all six windows.

I didn't carry my pistol on me considering I wasn't with this life anymore, I felt it wasn't needed, but one thing for sure is I never got rid of it I just put it away, but from the looks of it that was the wrong idea.

As I got closer to the car and I stood there not knowing who was in the car. I didn't jump, I didn't react. If they wanted me dead they would have been shot at me.

Using my finger I signaled them to roll down the window, soon as I did that they rolled it down just a little. As I tried looking inside to see who it was the driver sped off leaving behind nothing but smoke and black tire marks.

I didn't have time to be playing these mind games with these niggas, if they wanted me they knew exactly where to find me. Niggas couldn't wait until I came home. Whatever it is they had against me I was prepared for anything. I knew the beef wasn't gone be completely over once I touched down.

Rock

The sun was shining right through my window pissing a nigga off. I looked over to the left side of me and forgot I had Nicole ass in the bed with me. We weren't a couple but we had an understanding. She knew what was up and so did I, plus she had a son and I wasn't into playing step daddy to another nigga seed.

"Get up ma." I said smacking her on the ass.

"Ouch." She moaned.

"Spark up." I said climbing out the bed.

Getting out the bed I walked into the direction of my bathroom to piss, brush my teeth and wash my face. Feeling the aches in my back I had to be tearing some shit up last night.

Finishing in the bathroom, I heard dishes raddling around so I made my way to the kitchen and found lil mama in there getting ready to cook breakfast. I could use something like her around more often, but I doubt if that happened.

"I hope it's good." I said teasing her.

"It's better than this." she said pointing to her pussy.

"Owee ma, you nasty." I flirted back.

Walking in my room getting ready to smoke, I checked my phone and seen Slim sent me a text saying to hit his line when I got up. He was an early bird and I wasn't.

"Yo?" I said into the phone once he picked it up.

"Man some weird shit just happened." He said.

"Like what? You good?" I asked sounding curious.

"Yea, shit cool this way. But nigga, I was coming home from Walmart and I noticed a car was sitting in front of the house. I walked towards the car and told them to roll the window down and they did just a little but I didn't see a face and then they drove off. Crazy huh?" he explained.

"I wonder what that was about. I know you aint into this shit anymore but it's time you carry that pistol with you." I said meaning everything I said.

"I feel you, but I'm gone hit you up later dawg." He said hanging up.

Slim and I been best friends since we were younger, grew up right next door to each other, so I would never in my life cross him. We had more than a friendship, we was more like brothers.

I respected him for leaving the streets alone and I will never stop associating with him because he chose a different path then me. He was gone always be my dawg no matter which walk of life he chose.

Me personally, leaving the streets was something I could never do, getting money every day and night was my specialty and I did this shit in my sleep. I was made for the streets and that was something I didn't have a complication with.

I always stayed out late nights on a money mission. Sometimes I never had time to sleep. I had nobody to come home to, so I spent most of my time in the streets doing business and making sure shit was looking how it was supposed to.

Staring out the window, it was a good ass day and I thought about hitting Slim back up to see if he wanted to throw something on the grill. Receiving his response, he said it was good with him but we needed to do things at his house because he had the biggest.

Looking at the time, it was still early so I didn't plan on getting dressed until two. Smoking my blunt and looking at the T.V. I noticed lil mama was coming in the room with two plates in each hand. I ain't gone lie the shit smelled and looked good. A nigga loved a woman who can cook especially some breakfast and soul food. She walked over with nothing but her boy shorts on and one of my tee-shirts.

"Thanks ma." I said reaching for my food.

"You're welcome." She said.

Looking down at the plate she fixed a nigga some cheesy eggs with toast, bacon and sausages with some grits on the side and a cup of apple juice. I ate every crumb within two minutes.

"Was it good or were you just hungry?" she asked noticing the way I had cleaned up my plate in a matter of time.

"It was good." I said.

She picked up our plate and headed back into the kitchen. I watched her ass jiggle in her shorts causing lil man to stand up wanting some attention. Mann! Sitting on my bed smoking another blunt I picked up my phone and saw a picture message from a chick I use to fuck with her pussy all over the screen. You will never be wifey doing shit like that.

I texted Moe ass and told him about the cook-out that we was having, if he came he did if not oh well. Since Slim told Moe he was done with the streets he started to get distant but I didn't take shit personal and I didn't give a fuck because I was still a money machine with him or without him.

I jumped out the bed and went in the bathroom to hop in the shower. Making sure the water was real hot, I rinsed off my body first and then soaped up my towel making sure I washed up about five times.

"I'm leaving boo." She yelled in the bathroom.

"Okay cool. Lock the door." I yelled back.

Jumping out the shower I grabbed my towel and dried off. Walking out the bathroom I was walking around killing time. I went in the living room in sparked me up a blunt. I couldn't go a day without smoking; this was a hobby to me.

Looking around I was always satisfied with my crib. I had a 2 bedroom 2 bath apartment that was big enough for me. My living room had two all-black sectionals with the big red fluffy pillows. Along with the tile flooring, white and crème walls, with a 55 inch Flat that hung up on the wall and a white and black area rug with an all-white table. On the wall were pictures of my mom and my big mama.

Entering my room I snatched the sheets and covers off my bed so I could change them; I pulled out my brand new Ralph Lauren bed set and fixed up my bed. . After I was done I started looking through my closet, I thought about rocking my all-whites shoes, black True Religion jeans, and my white tee, and of course some Jewelry had to go around my neck and wrist. Clothes were nothing to me, I wasn't the flashy type; I was a typical tee-shirt and blue jeans kind of nigga.

Thinking about the bbq, I was hoping Jasmine was gone bring her home girl with her. She was bad as fuck to me, the kind of girl I found myself fucking with the long way. She played too many games for me though and we were both grown as hell. When I saw her back at the club I knew I wanted her, but once I noticed she was boo'd up with another nigga I told myself I'll get her another time. I just wanted to get to know her and what she was about. Shorty was use to fucking with lames, but once she starts fucking with a real nigga she'll be sprung within seconds.

I wasn't too sold with the idea of having a steady relationship, especially at a time like this, I just couldn't dig it. I wasn't a dog or nothing but I loved the streets too much to have a girl at home. If we both got an understanding that we just chillin, nothing more and nothing less than that was good. Some bitches wanted a lil too much, once you start giving her the dick she feel like she own yo ass. Nah boo! Me and Nicole just kept each other occupied until further notice. I didn't expect things to go far with her because she was a hood bitch herself.

I mean don't get me wrong a wifey type of female is a good thing but if I be out here all night and day she gone be thinking I'm somewhere fucking off and I ain't got time for that insecurity shit.

Money was who I was married to she don't fuss, be insecure or none of that shit so I was happy with her.

Growing up as a young nigga I didn't see too much money, my mother was married to a busta who'd rather trick with hoes then feed his child. I was the only child and after me my pops told her he didn't want any more kids. Even though my mom always dreamed of having a big family, she did what he said because she felt like she needed him.

He knew exactly what he was doing; he was the one bringing in the big money while she was working a part time job at the Laundry Matt. When I turned fifteen, I got tired of seeing my mom worrying, crying and stressing about the shit he was putting her through. I got tired of coming home to see eviction notices posted on the doors, seeing our fridge empty and furthermore, I hated when we had to heat up water in the microwave.

Some days I would be in my room and I'd hear how he basically made her trick with him to get money for the shit we needed. He was the definition of a dog and I hated his ass.

As I got older I realized waiting around for a check wasn't for me. When it came to me slaving for some weak ass $300 dollars every two weeks I wasn't motivated to do that.

When sixteen came around I got out here and made shit happen for me and my moms and told my dad we didn't need him for shit and he left us to be with somebody else. My mom was hurt and all she did was cry but I told her long as she keep taking him back to keep hurting her I wasn't gone deal with her either.

I lost my mom to cancer at the age of seventeen, matter fact the day of my birthday and after that I was on my own and never heard or seen from my father and I really didn't care. If he wanted to see me he would have been came and found me but being the kind of nigga he was he wouldn't care if I was dead or alive.

I always reminded myself to be better than he was. I would never allow myself to follow his footsteps. If God blessed me with a family I was gone make sure they didn't need and want for nothing.

Walking out the door I hit the alarm and got to the garage and hoped in my 2015 all-Red Charger with the red chrome rims and black tents.

I had them Doughboy Cash out Niggas blasting through my speakers. I fucked with they music heavy. They spoke some real shit about life, money, bitches and the struggle. When it came to struggles in life I was living proof of that and couldn't anybody tell me different.

Before going over to Slim crib I made my way to my trap spot that I had located on the East Side of town. To stop things from happening to my products and money I had the house fixed up nice. Not only was it looking nice, I used an older black couple to pretend they was living here and I made sure I paid them good. They had a life on their own but most of the times they'll end up staying here many nights. The job was dangerous but being that Mr. Jenkins was into this lifestyle back in his day he knew how everything went and he didn't let shit bother him.

The main floor of the home was set up like a normal house. The last floor which was the basement was split between different sections. I had a couple chicks bagging up dope, a couple young niggas packing it up and far left was two lil homies who would count the money.

Making sure everything was good and the amounts were right I paid each person fairly and made my way back upstairs. Walking out the front door I made my way to my car and drove off heading towards my destination.

Pulling up to the stop light I turned my head to the right and noticed a group of younger dudes that had to be like 10 or11 was standing at the corner pointing at my car.

Making a quick U-turn I pulled around and parked on the side of the street to where they were standing at.

"Y'all like what y'all see?" I asked.

"Yea man I wanna be like you when I grow up." One of them said.

"Naw son, you wanna be better than me. You like basketball?" I asked noticing the ball in his hands.

"Yes, I love it." He said dribbling the ball around.

"Follow your dreams boy; you can be anything you want in this world. Don't let nothing or nobody tell you different or mess that up." I said shaking his hand.

"What were your dreams?" he asked me.

The question threw me off a little, but I didn't hesitate or nothing I told him straight up.

"To be my own boss." I said

I took out three hundred dollars and handed them each a hundred dollar bill, with the expression on their faces I could tell they weren't use to it but I was in their shoes before and hopefully they take my advice.

"Woah, thanks man." One of the lil dudes said.

"No problem, go finish enjoying y'all day and remember what I said." I told them. Instead of them going to finish playing basketball they ran right past the court and ran up the street to a small convenient store. I hopped back into my car and headed to my next destination.

Pulling in the front of Slim crib I got out and hit the alarm button on my car. It was a selected few who knew where he lived which was a smart idea since you couldn't let everybody know where you laid your head at.

As I strolled to the backyard I saw Slim, his girl Jasmine and on the left of her was her home girl and man she had a nigga on hard the way her hips and ass was hugging that dress.

"Wassup everybody?" I said.

"Hey." said Jasmine.

"Hey." said her friend.

"Wasupp Nigga" laughed Slim.

Just by the look on my face he already knew what I was on. I never caught her name though but I bet you I get it before we leave tonight.

Thirty minutes later Moe walked in with a cooler and two bitches on his right and left side. I saw the way Jasmine turned her nose up once she laid eyes on the hoes he brought.

"Kema?" Jasmine said to one of the girls.

"Hey." She spoke back.

"What's good everybody?" asked Moe. Something was fishy about him he was acting too happy but I ignored it and focused on having a good time.

"Sup lil Nigga." I said, surprised that he actually showed up.

I walked inside the house and saw Jasmine friend staring a nigga down so that right there told me she liked what she saw. She quickly turned my frown upside down on some kiddy shit.

"Staring that hard ain't gone solve nothing." I said licking my lips.

"You had to be looking at me first to know I was staring." she flirted.

"Did you like what you saw?" I asked.

"Maybe." she said winking her eye.

"What's your name?" I asked,

"Lia, and yours?" she asked.

"Rodney, but everybody call me Rock." I said.

"Nice to meet you." she said and walked off.

Noticing she was trying to play hard to get I let it slide, I ain't gone chase her or kiss her ass. She was cute as hell though, but she will come around if she won't too I never begged a female to get their attention.

As I walked in the bathroom I heard a knock on the door and once I opened it I was staring at one of the chicks Moe had with him.

"Can't you see the bathroom occupied?" I asked her.

"Is that right?" she asked pushing me back inside.

She locked the door and instantly dropped to her knees. Now what nigga gone turn down some head? She was a straight hoe, wasn't no if, ands or buts about it. All Moe did was fuck around with nothing but hoes. She unzipped my pants and put her mouth on all 9 inches of my dick.

"Fuck lil mama." I groaned as she twirled around the tip of my dick. Then, she swallowed every inch of my dick including my balls.

Seconds later, I was releasing my seeds down her throat and she kept sucking like the champion she was. Once we came out the bathroom Lia was standing in the kitchen on the phone and ole girl turned around and shot her a smirk.

"Bitch." Said Lia.

"The baddest one." She said walking back outside.

I knew my chances of fucking with Lia was gone out the window. The look she had on her face when I came out read she wasn't fucking with me. I just shook my head and walked back outside.

"Nigga these hoes ain't shit." said Moe as he walked up to me.

"You already know?" I laughed.

"Hell yeah, I knew one of them was gone do some trife shit that's why I brought them. Bros for my hoes, but I didn't think Slim girl was gone be here. I thought it was gone be an orgy going on tonight." He laughed.

"You a fucking fool." I laughed back at his ass.

The night was winding down and a lot more people came than I thought would actually show up. Ace, one of my trap workers and his baby mama came through and Slim invited a couple of his neighbors over, they was some cool ass white people though. The older guy John was so turnt up off them jello shots Jasmine made. His wife came over a few times to get him but he wasn't paying her any attention.

It was time to go, well for the guests to go. I'm glad didn't shit happen so far but I had a gut feeling that something bad was about to, I wasn't sure what though.

"Aight niggas, I'm out. I got some pussy to tend to." Said Moe gathering up his hoes.

"Be easy nigga." I said laughing at his dumb ass.

"You rolling with me? You already got yo starter pack earlier." We all laughed including the hoe who sucked me up in the bathroom.

"Naw, I'm straight." I said back.

"Ain't nothing wrong with a little fun." Kema winked her eyes at me.

"Didn't he say he straight?" Snapped Lia. I looked at her and laughed, she wasn't fucking with a nigga in no kind of way but she had the nerve to speak once she seen lil mama trying to invite me to her slumber party.

She kept staring at me the rest of the night but words never left her mouth. I knew she wanted me but I wasn't gone hound her. In a matter of time, she'll be fucking with a nigga the long way.

I got ready to leave; I was tired and had to get up in the morning because I had some business to handle. I said goodbye to everybody and made my way towards the door, soon as I opened the door I was being pushed back in by two dudes with a pistol in my face, between my eyes.

I already knew the consequences to this, somebody gone walk out here alive, dead, or limping. He still had the gun pointed towards my head; I wasn't no punk when it came to a nigga pulling a gun out on me. It's either you gone use it or you ain't, but I promise you if I was you I would use it because soon as I get lose I'm killing yo ass.

"We can make this easy or hard, it's y'all choice" said the dude.

"Hard way." said Slim.

"Where the shit at?" he asked.

"I 'on keep shit in my house." said Slim.

"Who sent y'all?" I asked.

"Do you think I'm dumb enough to tell you?" he laughed.

Little did they know we could find out sooner than he thought. It didn't take a rocket scientist to figure out shit. I have been put it worse situations than this and still came out on top.

I can see that Lia and Jasmine was scared, I noticed Lia kept winking her eye at me but I didn't know what she was trying to tell me. I slid my hands in my pocket, reaching for my gun. I couldn't speak to her, so I just stood there looking at her.

"Don't even think about it." he said.

"Which one of y'all is Jasmine?" the other one asked.

"Who wants to know?" asked Slim.

"Look at you tryna be captain save a hoe." He laughed.

"Just know he said he got his eye on you and your bitch." The other dude said.

Jasmine looked confused, hell we all were clueless. You can tell these niggas wasn't about shit because both of them had pistols but neither one of them let them bitches bark.

Jasmine snatched a knife out her purse and sliced it across one of the dude's ankle causing him to fall giving me time to pull my gun out. I aimed it in the other dude direction the same time he had his gun pointed at me.

"One of us I gotta die." He said.

"Which one it's gone be?" I asked

POW! POW! POW!

"Oh my gosh." cried Jasmine.

Lia

I was use to this kind of shit dealing with the wrong niggas. I was making eye contact with Rock when the dude had his gun pointed at him but I could tell he didn't understand me. When I see my life in danger I 'on mind shooting or stabbing me a mutha fucka so I did what I had to do.

I don't even know why I allowed myself to get jealous when Rock came out the bathroom with that hoe. I felt like shit and he wasn't even my man. When I saw her smirk at me that was the ticket that unleashed my attitude. I was embarrassed because I wasn't supposed to feel this way towards a nigga who wasn't mines.

The whole ride home was quiet. Jasmine wasn't talking, she was still frightened. Slim told her plenty of times she had nothing to worry about but since the things happened with Kenny she was still nervous.

Pulling up to my place we got out the car and Slim came around to say his goodbyes to Jasmine.

"Look at me ma." He said as he lifted her head up to face him. "I got you baby, around me you'll always be safe. Now give me a kiss." He said pulling her close to him.

"Thanks baby." She said still traumatized.

"I'm gone see you later right? He asked her.

"Yes." She said softly.

"I'll have your car here before you open your eyes in the morning." He said. They kissed again and for the first time I was glad that she had finally found someone who loved her for her.

Rock got out the back and hopped into the front seat looking at me like he wanted something. I waved bye and that was all. An attitude was written all over my face, for what reason I didn't know.

We made it inside the house and I checked around making sure everything was okay before we got comfortable. Once I noticed everything was the same I walked into my room.

***

Sitting in the tub relaxing my body Rock was heavy on my mind. Just thinking about him made me crème off rip.

He stood about 5"9 creamy brown skin with a nice hair cut that he wore in a low fade but you were still able to see the thick waves he had. Another thing that was breathtaking was those deep dimples, and he had the prettiest smile I had ever seen on a dude. I was playing hard to get, something I didn't do often. I knew nothing about him but from what I saw today proved to me that was is a hoe.

My phone started ringing and flashing across the screen was a number I haven't seen before.

"Hello?" I answered.

"You don't know what you done got yourself into." they said.

The caller hung up the phone and that shit scared the fuck out of me. It wasn't because of what they said, but the person voice just sounded unreal, something you would hear in a horror movie. For the moment I thought it was Twan. That voice was too similar to his but I could have been tripping from all the blunts I smoked earlier.

Speaking of Twan, I haven't seen him since the night at the club. We've talked and texted over the phone but nothing serious. I wanted to get to know him a little more than what he told me at the club. He asked to take me out a couple times, but I always lied saying I had something to do.

Hopping out the bath, I dried off and wrapped up in my robe. Looking in the mirror I started to fix my hair. This red was starting to get old so I was dying for something new. I had to make an appointment with my girl Nicole. She was the only one I let put her hands in my head.

Jasmine was in the shower cleaning herself up and as of now I could use some drinks, so I wanted to know if my girl was up for going to the mini bar around the corner. I needed something strong to release the stress off my back tonight.

"You okay?" I asked walking in the bathroom.

"Yeah boo I'm good." she said.

"Are you up for a drink tonight?" I asked.

"We can go but make sure you grab your pocket knives." she said looking so serious. I laughed at her because she knew she didn't have to tell me.

The only thing that seemed to calm me down was liquor and some dick on the side but being single, I had no choice but to satisfy myself tonight. Since I had that bad situation with Donte, I wasn't giving my goodies up to nobody but my unnatural dicks.

Walking into my room I looked in my night stand that I called "The bad girl stand" where I had condoms, lubricant, vibrators, dildos, my hand gun, pocket knives, mace and some handcuffs.

When it came to me protecting myself I made sure I had everything by me at all times since there was cray people in this city.

Dressed in some Rocks jeans, an all-white Nike shirt with some Jordan's on my feet I was ready to go. Following behind me

Jasmine had on her all-white Nike Air Max shoes with the NIKE jogging suit to match.

Making our way out the house we both looked over our shoulders making sure the coast was clear. We wasn't the type to call the police if something went down we was the ones to take action right on the spot.

"Everything seems good boo." She said.

"Yeah let's go." I said

Jumping into my white 15' Chevy Camaro SS I sped off in silence heading to D'Js. It was around midnight so I'm sure the bar was jumping and that's why I had all my kill a bitch shit with me because I wasn't up for playing games with anybody.

Pulling up to the bar I noticed there wasn't too many cars which was a good thing since all we wanted to do was get buzzed and go back home.

Walking inside the bar me and Jasmine both took notes of all the faces remembering everything that we needed to. None of the faces here looked familiar, so we were good.

"What you want to drink? It's on me?" she asked.

"Get me my favorite girl." I said watching my surroundings. Only thing I drunk was Hennessey and Coke.

Watching as Jasmine told the bartender our orders I looked over towards the back and noticed a familiar face. Double checking, I had to make sure I got the right woman. Sipping my drink I rolled my eyes not paying her any attention.

"Girl, that's Donte wife over there." I pointed over to the lady. He didn't have a young one, he had him some old meat who had to be anything over 30.

"Really? Is that why she kept staring over here?" she asked.

"Yeah that's the bitch, I want her to say something she gone get her ass whipped in here tonight." I snapped.

We was on drink number three already and I was feeling myself. Donte wife kept eyeing me and I was so close to approaching her but I'm gone let her mad ass slide. It ain't my fault I was what her man wanted. The shit was over and done with, but if she wanted to keep it going we can because I don't mind making a bitch who don't like me hate me even more.

Making our way to the dance floor I was switching my hips and ass back and forth, I was bound to show my ass tonight just to give the bitch something to stare at. She could never do the things I did because if that was the case, her man wouldn't be blowing up my line daily.

"Girl, look there goes Donte" she said.

I looked up and saw him take a seat by his wife. I didn't understand why he lied and said they weren't together because I could care less about their relationship. Why did he lie? I could really give two fucks.

Snapping me out my thoughts two handsome fellas approached us asking if we wanted to dance.

Perfect timing. I thought to myself.

I knew he was over there in his feelings because Donte was in love with my ass. Not forgetting what he did, I knew I couldn't run back to that.

The DJ had TI song *No Mediocre* blasting through his speakers and since I had a fat ass, I made sure both cheeks were glued to his dick.

*"All I fuck is bad bitches
I don't want no mediocre
Don't want no mediocre
I don't want no mediocre, no
Bad bitches only
Ain't no mediocre
Don't want no mediocre."*

"What's yo name ma?" he asked.

"The name is Lia and yours?" I said.

"Stew boo." He said.

"You got a man? Shit I 'on even know why I asked cause I really could care less if you was taken or not." He said.

"Is that right?" I flirted.

"Hell yeah, you bad as fuck." He said.

"Thanks Stew." I said twisting and shaking my ass.

I really wasn't interested in this dude. I mean the dance was good, but all I could smell was weed and liquor on his breathe and that turned me off. He looked like a basic nigga with no jewelry or nothing and that was a turn off too. Making the conversation and dance short I told him my feet was hurting.

Finishing our dance, I walked away and saw Donte walking towards me but this time his wife was nowhere to be found. If I didn't hate his ass, I'd dance all over his dick just to get him horny and then play his ass to the left. Niggas hate that shit, getting them all hard and ready to fuck then play they ass like dude on that Facebook video "GOT EMMMMM".

"What you doing Lia?" he asked.

"What do you mean?" I asked.

"Don't act stupid, you think I'm blind, like I don't see you in here tossing yo ass all up on these broke ass niggas remember you gone always mine." he snapped.

"What I do is not your concern, last time I checked you had a wife. Does she know you all in my face and shit? I snapped.

"Man I sent her ass home, don't keep fucking playing with me." he said.

"You had your chance and fucked it up, we was never in a relationship anyway, so I don't need you coming over here yelling and shit like you my man. What we had is over, matter of fact get the fuck away from me." I yelled walking off.

He grabbed me by my arm and I slapped the shit out of him. Jasmine came out of nowhere hitting him with a two-piece like she was fighting a bitch in the streets.

"Have you lost your fucking mind?" I asked snatching away.

"Keep fucking with me you gone lose yo life." he screamed.

"You better watch yo back." said Jasmine.

"Is that a threat?" he said walking up to her.

"I ain't scared to fight a nigga. Come on Lia, I clearly don't have time and neither do you." She said yanking on my arm.

The security guard was already on his way towards us but there really was no need for him because we were already leaving.

"Is you ok?" asked Jas.

"Yeah girl I'm fine." I said.

"This has been a fucked up day for us." I said.

"You ain't never lied, I just need to go home and pop two Tylenols and sleep the night away." She said.

Pulling out the parking lot Jas phone buzzed letting her know she was receiving a text. The way she was smiling I could tell it was from somebody she wanted to talk to.

"What's the Kool-Aid smile for?" I asked being nosey.

"That was Slim telling me my car was parked at your house." She said.

"And what else? Because I know that didn't have you smiling like that." I laughed.

"He said he missed me bitch DAMN." She said.

"My bad sistah girl, don't get all jazzy." I laughed.

We pulled up to my house, Jas asked if I needed her to stay here with me but I didn't I was a big girl and I damn sure wasn't worried about Donte or his bitch. If they knew better, they wouldn't bring their asses to my house.

"You sure you don't need me?" she asked sounding concerned.

"No girl I'm fine boo. If I do I'll call." I said.

"Ok. Love you." she said.

"Love you too, call me when you get home." I said walking inside the house.

First thing I wanted to do was take me another long bath, sip some wine and play me some music all night. I got inside my house cut the lights on, and started to check my house just in case anything seemed suspicious, but good thing it didn't because I had enough drama tonight.

Going into my bedroom I stopped in the mirror and thought to myself Girl you beautiful. I was in love with myself and there was nothing anybody could do to stop that.

Running me some bath water I started to think about how me and my parent's relationship would be. I always wished I knew them, and knew what they were like. If my mom was anything like me then she was a killa. My father? I just wished my nana told me something before she had to leave this world.

I sat in the tub thinking about how I wish things would have been differently in my life but growing up a young confused girl like me you tend to attach yourself to anything just to feel loved by anything and anybody, not wanting to be alone.

Snapping me out my lonely thoughts I was receiving a call from Jas, my girl was worried about me but she know I'll cut a mutha fucka up in a minute. But then again it feels good to have someone on your side when it seemed like the whole world was against you.

"Wassup boo?" I answered.

"I made it home, what you doing?" she asked.

"Sitting in this tub, what you doing honey?" I asked.

"Girl, the same thing. I needed to relax my body. Today has been a stressful, crazy ass day." she said.

"Yeah you right about that." I said.

"You working tomorrow?" she asked.

"Girl yes, you?" I asked.

"You know I am." she said.

"Hold on girl, somebody is blowing my phone up." I said.

"Just call me tomorrow." she said.

"Okay boo." I said.

"I love you bestie. She said sounding sentimental.

"I'm gone be fine girl and I love you more." I said.

I hung up the phone from with her and when I saw who was calling me I instantly rolled my eyes and hit ignore on my phone. Thinking it would do something but it didn't, my phone kept ringing.

"What Donte?" I yelled.

"Man, open the door." He said.

"What? Why are you here?" I asked.

"What you mean? I'm home and ready to lay down."

I burst out laughing through the phone, this nigga was on some drugs or some shit because he really thought we were still fucking around and that was never the case. I needed to be high like him hell, cause whatever it was that was some good shit.

"This isn't your home and why don't you get the point I'M DONE." I said screaming through the phone.

I hung up the phone, and soon as I set the phone down I heard two gun shots right in front of my house. Picking up the phone and it was Donte calling me again.

"What the fuck just happened?" I yelled getting out the tub.

"Open the damn door I'm not playing with you." He said.

"Mannnn, you crazy as hell here I come dude." I said.

Walking to the door with my robe on I could hear the police sirens coming and I hoped and prayed they didn't come to my house. It was dark out so I'm sure they didn't see him at my front door.

"Perfect timing." He said.

"What you say that for?" I said rolling my eyes.

"Bend over." He said.

"Un UN nigga, you is not finna put your dirty dick inside me." I yelled pushing him away from me.

He pushed me on the couch, trying to fight him off me but his extra strong ass wasn't buying it.

He flipped me over to where my ass was towards the ceiling and soon as I tried to move away he shoved his tongue inside my pussy from the back.

"Stoppppppp." I moaned.

I wasn't trying to let him hear me moan but hell I couldn't help it. Donte always had some fye head and he knew it. He did it with so much pride.

"Damn. Stop fighting it ma, you know you want this." he said sticking his finger in my ass.

That's the thing with these dudes and when they mess up. Fucking with someone heavy they find out your weaknesses and know what to do to get you back right with them. They always come kissing your ass with head and when they do it they do it like an angel sent them to do the job.

The way he was vibrating his tongue on my clit made my juices poor out of me like water and I couldn't hold back any longer.

"Oh my fucking god….." I yelled. Donte was vibrating his tongue against my clit like he was in a pussy eating contest.

The moans that were coming from my mouth seemed unreal, I didn't even know what I was saying. I was moaning like I was a Chinese girl or something.

"Shit… I'm cumin……" I said.

Boyyy! Yes, I missed his head it's been a long time since I had it and at this moment I didn't want it to leave. He laid down on the side of me and if he thought I was gone put my mouth to work on his dick he had another thing coming. He had me all the way messed up.

"Thanks for the head." I laughed.

"Girl….." he said.

"I know you aren't waiting for something in return?" I asked.

"Girl nawl, just go to sleep." He said.

What the hell? This nigga just came over here to eat my pussy then go to sleep? Um, I can dig it. Donte had something up his sleeves and I couldn't wait to find out what it his he was hiding. Tomorrow I will be making an appointment to get checked out, he had me fucked up.

***

The next morning I rolled over to an empty bed which was fine with me. Getting out the bed I headed to the bathroom to handle my morning hygiene. I was hoping Nicole didn't have any appointments in the next hour or two because I needed my hair touched up.

Soon as I was done in the bathroom, I grabbed my purse and headed out the door. Hopping in my car I was in awe. I always wanted to drive a fast car when I got older and now that I got one it made me feel like one of them wild bitches, who had a body covered in tattoos that had a thing for race cars. Moments later I pulled up to the hair salon and didn't see any cars.

"Hey girl." she spoke as I entered.

"Hey, you don't have any appointments do you?" I asked.

"Nope you right on time." she said.

"What I'm doing for you today?" I pulled out my phone and showed her a hairstyle I been dying to get. It was a bright chick like me with purple hair.

"You got me?" I asked her.

"You already know this bitch." We both laughed as she started on my head.

I was getting another short bob, but this time my right side was gone be longer. I always walked out satisfied when she blessed my head. Nicole knew what she was doing when it came to slaying some weave.

She was a hair stylist and a hood ass bitch who I fucked with. We didn't hang or anything like that but she was still cool. Everything about her was low-key, she didn't tell anybody her business not even her own family. Whoever she was fucking around with had to be that nigga because she was a bad bitch. All I knew was she had a two year old son and her baby daddy was murdered a couple years ago.

"How ya girl been doing?" she asked referring to Jasmine.

"She's been good girl."

"That's good haven't seen her in a long time." She said back.

She finished working on my head and we were almost done. While I was sitting here my phone rung and it was Twan calling me.

"Hello." I answered.

"What's good ma, what you up to?" he asked me.

"Nothing, just getting my hair done, that's it. What you doing?"

"Out catching plays you know how that goes."

"Cool, I'll hit you up once I leave here and maybe we can get into something later on." He agreed and we hung up.

"Yesssssss bitch." She yelled.

She turned me around facing the big mirror she had hanging on the wall. She did her damn thing once again.

"You got me on fleek." I laughed.

"Only you boo. You know I always gotta do extra in your head." She said back.

I paid her the money while she did my eyebrows and after that I was heading out the door. My appointment wasn't until another hour so I decided to stop and get me something to eat from Chicken Coop.

***

Walking inside the doctor's office I signed in and sat down waiting for the assistant to come out and call my name so I could get this over and done with. Looking at my surrounding's I saw a lot of young girls in here with pregnant bellies, sitting alone. Some was crying while the other ones were taking pictures of their belly as if they were happy to be pregnant. If you ask me, I would say neither one of these girls was older than 17, shaking my damn head.

"Lia O'Neal?" said the lady standing by the door. I got up and followed her to the back. She checked my weight and height, and we walked into the room.

"You have to pee in this cup for Me." she said handing me the cup and wipe.

"Okay." I said. I walked out and made my way to the bathroom. Once I filled the cup up to the line, I wiped myself and got up. Washing my hands, I headed out the bathroom. As I made it back in she asked me a few questions until my doctor came in to check me.

"Here are your results." She said as she handed me my paperwork. Reading over everything, I did nothing but close my eyes.

Slim

It's been a week since I had seen or talked to Jasmine, last time we talked she said she had a lot going on with work and school, and last time I saw her was when that incident happened at my crib.

I hoped shorty wasn't blowing me off because of that, if so it was understandable because it all happened too fast.

I couldn't think about her leaving me alone. I didn't even get the pussy yet and I was already whipped. Jasmine was so different then other chicks I came in contact with. She was down to earth and very outgoing. She never asked me for anything and she handled her business well, like a women was supposed to. For her to be only twenty two she had older women beat, because she was on her shit.

I started getting comfortable around her and I knew a lot about her just by spending time with her. She didn't like to sleep with the lights on, she loved sleeping cold, she hated sleeping without pillows and every time she get mad or irritated she would get quiet on me and go to playing with her finger nails.

I didn't know if it was love or lust but every time I saw Jasmine or thought about her it sent chills down my body and she always kept a nigga smiling. I didn't expect Jasmine to be anything like Princess.

Jasmine is very different and I love that. I'm glad she knew nothing about the streets, and I was upset with myself when that shit happened at my crib because I didn't want her to think we did shit like that. I shared things with her from my past and told her the old me would never come back unless someone was fucking with my loved ones.

Searching through my contacts I decided to give her a call to see how she was doing or if she needed anything.

"Hello?" she answered.

"Damn, it's like that ma?" I asked.

"No, I'm sorry I just been so busy with work and school." she said.

"That's cool, I ain't mad at you. How's it's going for you?" I asked.

"It's good, just so much work she gives us. I'm free today wassup?" she said.

"We can go out tonight sometime, if that's okay." I asked sounding like a bitch.

"Fine, I'll be ready around 9." she said.

"That's perfect." I said.

Since it was still early I was gone ride to my youth center and check on my staff and everybody else. I try to teach the kids different things everyday so they would grow up and do shit different then what I did. Since I really can't teach a girl anything I thought about having Jas go down there to talk to them some days. Everything was going good my way and I was proud of myself. I never thought I had the heart to do anything like this just because I was a cold-blooded nigga.

My restaurant and club was doing numbers. I made sure I thanked every customer or guest for coming by. The people that were hired were doing a good job by treating them with respect and satisfying theur every need.

Riding down the street looking at all these fast food restaurants was making me hungry. I needed me a girl at home who didn't mind cooking for they man. I pulled up to McDonalds drive thru and ordered me three double cheeseburgers, two large fries, and a large coke.

"You have a good day sir." She said.

"Thanks ma, you have a good day too." I flirted winking my eye at her.

I really didn't have anything against a female working at McDonald's, Burger King or whatever. Money is money and you gotta get it how you can. Everybody wasn't built for the same shit so people got it, how they could. When you got responsibilities and shit to do you don't give a fuck how you hustle because at the end of the day don't nobody have you like you got yourself.

Pulling up to my youth center I saw all the young boys out playing basketball. One of the familiar faces was Ant. He was here every day; helping me out with things I needed done. Something told me he didn't have a real family at home so I always talked with him about certain things. Even when he would work for me I would pay him under the table, to keep money in his pocket, hoping it would stop him for entering the streets for money.

"What's good Ant." I said.

"What's up?" He said.

"Come hoop with us." he said passing me the ball.

"Y'all ain't ready." I laughed.

"Yeah right we are young and better." They said throwing their hands up, sharing laughter.

I showed them a few of my moves and they taught me a few of theirs.

Now that I was done playing with the boys I was headed inside of the place. This amazing 29,000 square feet youth center had a basketball court, theatre room that was decorated with the color red and white everything, a study room that included six big orange square shaped tables and white comfy chairs with a nude color tile on the floor. Hanging on the walls were quotes about life, pictures of important people and events. Last but not least it also included a Children's craft room, a small kitchen, computer room and two bathrooms.

I hired a personal cook.. During the interview session he told me he loved cooking for people and being around children, so I knew this was the right place for him to be. Another worker was Ms. Latisha who was hired for housekeeping. She was an alcoholic back in her days and ended up losing custody of her child, her only daughter. I made sure both workers got paid very well, also making sure their homes were taken care of.

Heading back outside, I checked around for the girls and didn't see any of them. When I got further out I noticed some commotion coming from the parking lot and once I got there it looked like a fight was getting ready to break off so I ran over to see what was going on. Once I got over I noticed it was Keisha and Kanisha arguing again.

"Stop this right now." I said grabbing Keisha.

"Bitch I'm beating yo ass when he leave." Yelled Kanisha.

"What's the problem?" I asked.

"She was talking shit, so I got in her face." Said Kanisha.

"Come inside so we can talk." I said demanding them both.

Sitting in the room with them both I could tell Keisha was nervous. She couldn't stop shaking or biting her finger nails. I brought them into here so we could get a better understanding and to note that this wouldn't happen again.

Besides her attitude I noticed she loved to sing and dance, and was very good at it because I saw it myself. She was a lost little girl who just needed someone to love and respect her and to show her how a woman should act and be treated.

"What's the problem?" I asked.

"She was talking about me so I got up ready to box." Said Kanisha.

"Don't lie on me, you called me a hoe." Said Keisha.

"You know it's not true." I said looking into her lost eyes.

"Shidddd, you must not know her." laughed Kanisha. This was a hot girl and needed one of those whippings my grandma handed my female cousins back in my day.

"Stop it." I said.

Finishing up our small talk I made them talk and shake each other hands hoping when I leave they wouldn't be fighting.

"I'm sorry." Said Kanisha.

"It's okay, me too." Said Keisha.

Making sure everything was going good with everyone I said my goodbyes and jumped in the car. I was now on my way to get ready for my date with Jasmine and I couldn't wait to see her beautiful smile.

Jasmine

Hearing the sound of my Sketchers squeaking across the marble flooring I was speeding through the halls of work, hurrying to clock out so I would have time to get ready for my date tonight with my man, Slim. I didn't want him thinking I was ignoring him; I just had a lot going on with my job and with school. This was the ending of this semester and I wanted to make sure my GPA stayed high.

"Jasmine dear you have a gift sitting on the registration desk out there." said the nurse walking past me.

Smiling, I knew it had to be Slim doing this because he was the only guy I was currently seeing and didn't have time for anyone else because I barely had time to share with him.

"I was told there's something up here for me." I said to the clerk.

"Yes dear the delivery man, dropped off some flowers for you." she said handing me my yellow and pink flowers.

Admiring the flowers I noticed a card was sticking out. As I picked it up there wasn't anyone name but it had a message.

I'll see you later bitch

I walked to the nearest trash and threw them in there without hesitating. Who could this be from? Who was after me? I can't lie I was afraid and nervous to even walk to my car.

***

Letting the phone ring, I was calling Lia to see if she wanted to come out and help me find something to wear but I got the voicemail so I figured she was working.

I pulled up to the lady boutique downtown. Hoping they would have something nice in here. I came in and the first thing I fell in love with was this blueberry short dress that will show half of my cleavage. I already had some all black heels at home with the matching purse, so I ended up grabbing the first thing I saw since I was already rushing.

Leaving the store I felt like I was being watched but I didn't pay any attention to it. As I looked around the parking lot the only car I seen was a white Dodge Dart that belonged to someone who I assumed was shopping too.

Pulling into my driveway I parked the car grabbed my bags and jumped out. Running up the steps, I checked the mailbox and noticed an envelope with my name on it but no address was shown.

Walking into the house I threw the envelope on the kitchen counter and walked towards my bathroom.

It was now 8:10 and boy time had been flying by so fast. Standing in the shower I allowed the water to run down my body allowing me to think about Kenny and the weird things I'd been receiving. If this is him after me, why did he wait so long to come find me? If he wanted me he shouldn't have waited this long, so it had to be another reason.

Stepping out the shower I grabbed my towel and ran into the room to quickly dry off. Standing in front of the fan I was hoping for a quick dry.

Once I got dressed I walked past the mirror and Idamn near wanted to have sex with myself before I left. I was looking amazing, but I just hoped Slim felt the same way once he saw me.

Standing here touching up my hair, I had a side part with my natural curls. Hugging my body was my short tight fitted strapless blue dress. On my feet was my all-black pumps with the purse to match. My silver jewelry danced around my neck and wrist. My full lips were coated with a nude color lipstick that I've recently bought.

I heard a knock on the door and the only person I was expecting was Slim and I prayed that was him because I wasn't up for any surprises.

"Wow." was all he said when I opened the door.

"What's wrong?" I asked thinking something was wrong with my attire.

"Man, you look good as hell in this dress." he said spinning me around to get a glance at everything I had on.

"Thanks love, you look handsome yourself." I said.

Seeing a man dressed in a suit was breath taking. His all-black Armani suit was looking good on him, looking like one of the men in black but he was standing alone. We got outside and he opened the door for me. Tonight he was pushing his all-black 2015 Mercedes Benz.

"You're perfect, just for me. Everything I wanted is right here." He said smiling, as he placed a soft kiss on my hand.

"Well thank you." I blushed.

Pulling up to his restaurant I was amazed how everything looked. There was nothing but blue lights surrounding the entire building. The dress I had on color coordinated perfectly with the beautiful decorations.

He stepped out the car and made his way to my side to open my door. Walking inside side by side I was really impressed how he had his restaurant decorated. The male workers wore white suites, and the female workers wore all-white dresses.

***

For the remainder of the night we talked and I found myself getting too comfortable with him. We laughed, joked around and even shared things from our past. It felt good to be in the presence of someone again, someone who adored you. I couldn't stop smiling or staring at this fine man who sat across the table from me.

The music in the background was so soft and calming. Putting me in mind of some good jazz music my dad use to listen to, oh how I miss that man.

"So why have you been single for so long?" he finally asked. I took a deep breath and thought about all the hurt and embarrassment I had in my past relationship.

"I've been scared of relationships since my last relationship because it's like you find yourself loving and caring for the wrong person when you knew for a long time that it wasn't right but you're just afraid to walk away. Why are you single?" I said shortening up my answer.

"I have my reasons, but I understand where you coming from with that one, commitment is a big and scary thing, but only if you're faithful and loyal and your partner isn't; but it's hard finding someone like that." He said.

I really wanted to know what his reasons behind that message were but he didn't seem like he was ready to tell me, but whenever he was ready to tell I was more than happy to listen.

I was more than satisfied with tonight. We danced twice and I was shocked that he knew how to slow dance, and good at that. Hood dudes could come with so many surprises, you just have to find that one who was raised by a queen and I found mine, salute to her.

Looking at the time I noticed we was so deep into each other that we were sitting here for at least three hours having the time of our life. For the first time, in a long time I was happy.

"Would you like to finish things back at my place?" he asked.

"Sure. I wouldn't want it any other way." I said. After the drinks, I was in my zone feeling myself. I felt like Slim got me drunk on purpose, but whatever reason that may be I was ready for it.

When I stood to my feet I had to catch my balance. I didn't want to seem wasted because of the fact that we were in public. He said his good-byes to his employees and we left.

Thirty minutes later we pulled up into his driveway and he helped me out noticing I was a little off balance.

"You had a little too much." He laughed.

"Oh. I'm fine." I lied. Too many shots of Tequila had me feeling myself a little too much.

On our way up to the door he took his mail out of the mailbox, and when we got inside he slung it across the living room table, just like I would do my mail.

He poured us both a glass of wine so we could finish what we started. It seemed like he was trying to get me wasted on purpose already knowing I was heading that way.

"Remember back at the restaurant I told you I had many reasons to be single?" He blurted out getting my attention. I was ready to hear everything he had to tell me. So I put my big girl panties on, hoping he wouldn't say he killed his ex or some crazy shit.

"Yes I do are you going to tell me?" I asked.

"I used to date this young lady name Princess, she was my first love and the only girl to ever have my heart. I was so over protective of her because of the lifestyle I was living. While I was locked up my homeboy told me someone had murdered her but I never found out who did it. I always told myself, when I do catch up with them they were dead." He said.

"I'm so sorry to hear that I know it was hard for you and still is if you need anyone to talk to I'm always here for you." I said.

Just by having someone by his side I knew would make him feel better. Dealing with stuff from your past you always need someone there for you.

I swear talking to him, seemed like we've known each other for years instead of months. This was the one for me and there was nothing or nobody who could mess this up.

"You mind telling me your reasons?" he asked sitting his drank down.

"Kenny cheated entirely too much for me. I did everything for him and when I say everything I mean every single thing. But one day I caught him cheating on me in the house we shared. That told me I needed to be done so I left for good and haven't seen him since, and that's why I've been afraid to love again." I said somewhat lying.

Even though I shortened my answer up I would feel awkward letting him know I killed a bitch over my supposed to be nigga.

"Damn baby girl, I'm sorry you got treated like that. Being that you're mines now you will never have to worry about that. Just don't fuck me over." He said. When he called me his, I wanted to smile from here to Florida.

"Losing her because of your lifestyle, is that the reason why you wanted to change your life around?" I blurted out.

"Yes it is. I mean I did my share of wrong and bad things, I'm not saying I'm perfect and what I did was right but I knew at that moment it was time to get right out here. I had the attitude like I'm the toughest nigga around town and shit couldn't happened to me or nobody could stop me. I promised myself would not live my life with that attitude anymore." He said.

"Thanks for the honesty, I really appreciate that." I said.

I loved his attitude and the way he kept it real with me. I laid in his arms staring into his eyes thanking God for placing me here.

"Come here and give me a kiss." He whispered in my ear sliding his tongue across at the same time.

"Long as you with me baby girl everything good." He said.

He stood up and told me to follow him to his bedroom and knowing how horny this liquor had me I did as I was told. Sticking his tongue in my mouth, I took the invite and welcomed it in.

"Ahhhhh, Slim baby that feels good" I moaned as he started sucking on my neck. He threw me on the bed and slid off my panties in the sexiest way ever.

The thought of controlling my body was out the window. I was inviting him into my personal life and was more than ready.

Throwing my head back, I laid there and let him do him. He had skills, demonstrating them like I was his boss and he had a point to prove.

"Ohh my gooosh," I moaned as he plunged his tongue deep inside me.

"You taste so good." He said making love to my pussy with his mouth.

"Ohh shit, I'm finna cum, I'm fuckingggg cumingggg" I moaned wrapping my legs around his neck.

I was good at giving head too, but when I tried to go down on him be pushed me back to the top so I climbed on top of him and slid my wetness on his dick and eased all the way down allowing myself to get comfortable with his ten inch dick. Remembering how frustrated I was, tonight I was taking my problems out on his dick.

"Fuckkk." he yelled while grabbing a hand full of my ass.

Chocking his dick with my pussy muscles I started bouncing making my ass clap all at once then I slowed up my speed and put my hands on his chest. Rotating my hips from left to right, I came up slowly and plopped back down.

"Damn girl, you a fucking beast." he moaned.

Throwing my left leg on top of the headboard while the other laid across his chest I bounced up and down making sure I felt every inch he had to offer. As I continued to twerk on his dick, I felt myself getting ready to release my juices.

"Let loose ma, don't hold it in." He instructed while switching positions. Placing me on all fours, he rammed his dick inside from the back. Holding on to my hips, I twerked on his dick as if I was on top of him. I was throwing my ass back matching his thrust. One thing he'll have to learn about me is that I fuck back.

"Hold on baby. Slow down." He moaned. I heard him but couldn't slow down, it was feeling to good and I was about to bust again.

"Shi-ttttt. I'm coming." He shouted as he released his seed deep inside of me. He groaned as he flipped me back over and collapsed on top of me. Both of us were trying to catch our breaths as we laid there.

Hours later he was lying next to me sleeping like a baby. "Put it on em make him wanna marry me" I sung to myself. I got up and made my way to his bathroom. Not knowing where he kept his clean towels I looked all over the bathroom to see if I could find something. I wanted to wake him, but I didn't know how he reacted to someone waking him out his sleep because that's one thing people don't play about.

After rambling in every draw I finally came across some wash towels and body towels. Turning the shower on, I made sure I got the water nice and hot before I got it. It's something about that hot water that relaxes your body.

Standing in the shower I couldn't believe I made myself comfortable in his home. With my own usage I felt like it wouldn't be a problem for me to wash off the bomb sex he just put on me.

Making sure my body was clean, I got out the shower and headed back to his room. From the looks of it he hasn't moved since I got out the bed. The hard part about not being in your own home, I didn't have anything to wear and I didn't want him thinking I was being nosey if I was to go inside his dresser.

Standing at the foot of the bed with my body towards his dresser I felt his hand on my shoulder.

"I see you made yourself comfortable." He said looking at my naked body.

"Mhm. I need something to wear; I didn't want to go inside your clothes. That's doing too much when I already invited myself in your shower." I laughed feeling embarrassed.

"Girl you're alright." He said climbing out the bed. He walked over and handed me one of his big t-shirts and some sheets to change the bed.

"I'm heading in the bathroom now, anything else you need just make yourself at home. I'm not selfish boo." He said walking out the room.

Once I got the fresh sheets on the bed, I looked inside the closet and grabbed a fresh cover. I grabbed my phone from my purse and jumped into the bed.

Laying in the bed playing candy crush, I was interrupted by a smell that I figured was his Gucci Body wash. Once I followed the smell he was standing by the bedroom door with nothing on. The way that water dripped down his body made me horny again.

"You like what you see ma?" he asked flexing his muscles.

"Mh-hmm." I hardly could respond. Staring at him I didn't know what to say, I was lost for words. Slim knew he was a breath of fresh air.

He dried off with the towel he grabbed and walked over to his dresser and threw on some boxers. Climbing into the bed, I turned around and he laid behind me and wrapped his arms around me, holding on to me. Right about now I knew for sure I didn't want to be alone anymore. Being in the arms of a man I felt secure. I knew being around him all the time I was safe from everything around me, and I didn't want to have it any other way.

Happiness was written all over my face, I'm glad I met someone so I could get over Kenny lying ass. I felt like I was falling in love all over again, I didn't know whether that was a good thing or a bad thing, but whatever life throws at me I'm willing to work with it. I always wanted to feel special to someone and that's the feeling Slim gave me. I had to stop blaming myself for Kenny's actions.

I'm stronger because I had to be, I'm smarter because of my mistakes, happier because of the sadness I stumbled over and now I'm wiser because of the lessons I learned. Life will teach you a lot about people and certain situations and all we could do is go with the flow.

"Goodnight baby girl." he said.

"Goodnight." I said back.

I knew I needed to be sleep for class in the morning but lying in his arms just had me feeling some type of way. Right about now, I would have been calling Lia to vent to her but I'll wait until; we have our girl's night out.

Lia

I was the happiest woman on earth when my doctor confirmed that I don't have any diseases. Even though I was clean, I still wasn't messing with Donte. He did it before so I'm sure he'll do it again and I wasn't about to get caught up with his bullshit again. I didn't even expect for him to give me some head. It happened so fast that I didn't have time to tell him to stop.

It's been some weeks since the last time I spoke with my bestie and I wasn't cool with that at all. I was happy she found somebody that appreciated her but damn.

Picking up my phone I went through my contacts and clicked on her name. I just wanted to see how things been going with her, but since I hadn't heard from her I figured they were good.

"Hello?" she answered.

"Damn remember me bitch?" I snapped.

"Boo it's nothing like that." she laughed.

"Yeah okay." I said.

"Love you more." she said.

"So what's been up thot?" I asked.

"Nothing girl, same stuff, what's been up with you?" She asked me.

"Nothing girl, I been kicking it with Twan." I said.

"You know I'm not feeling that right. That's Kenny old best friend and I wouldn't put shit past him, you need to fuck with Rock; he wants you." She said.

"How you know?" I smiled through the phone.

"He always asks me about you, give him a chance and get with him."

"Girl you know I ain't with all that commitment shit, I mean he is the only dude I'm fucking with at the moment, but I can't do relationships, I see him when I see him you know me if you ain't got no money or benefitting me what you in my face for?" I laughed but I was more than serious.

"Girl don't say it like that, I'm just saying you need to be trying to settle down with someone and stop chasing them dog ass dudes." she snapped back.

"Jasmine, you know I ain't with all that shit you talking about, hell I'm just trying to get me, listen baby love never paid the bills and money never cheated on me so why give these unfaithful ass niggas a chance to leave me heartbroken in the end and out in the cold. They don't give a fuck about yo feelings all they trying to do is lay-up with you and go fuck the next bitch, so that's why I do what I do, you can never run game on a bitch who been the coach. Rock got too much going on." I spoke the truth.

"Girl let me call you back in a second." She said. I knew she was feeling some type of way about what I said but she knew I was telling nothing but the truth. If God wanted me to settle down, he'll send me a good man.

We hung up and a message from Twan had come through, him asking if he could stop by and I said yes. I liked Twan a lot, don't get me wrong he's not perfect and neither is Rock but Twan never showed me his hoe side unlike Rock.

Jumping in the shower making sure the water was real hot and steamy; I climbed in and rinsed my body off. I couldn't see how females had no intentions on keeping their hygiene together. That was the most important thing in life.

Hopping out the shower I dried off and walked into my room. Looking through my closet I grabbed out my brand new Victoria's Secret lingerie with the matching robe. Rubbing my Very Sexy body lotion on my legs I made sure to lotion everything.

I dabbed a little perfume on my neck and wrist and sprayed some on my clothes and between my legs.

Thirty minutes later, Twan texted me and told me he was on the way. Walking into the kitchen, I poured me a shot of Hennessey and turned on some music. Once, I got back into my bedroom I heard a knock on the door.

Grabbing my gun out the kitchen draw I heard my phone ringing. Focusing on the attention from the other side of my door I didn't pay attention to the name on my phone so I just picked up the phone.

"Open the door." He yelled through the phone.

"Donte? What do you want?" I asked.

"Just to talk, nothing like that." he said.

"Donte I can't do that." I said.

"Come on man, I won't be long." he said. I opened the door and let him in, he looked me up and down and rolled his eyes.

"Are you planning on fucking him?" he asked. How did he know about someone coming over here? What was he on?

"What do you want?" I asked. The way he was looking at me I could tell that he'd been drinking. His eyes were glossy and blood shot red. It started to scare me but I wasn't about to let him see me sweat.

"So you cheating on me?" he asked walking towards me.

"Cheating? Boy is you dumb or something, I could have sworn you were married and we wasn't in a relationship." I snapped.

"But you know you want me as much as I want you." he said.

"Just leave Donte." I said pushing him back towards the door.

"So are you fucking him or not?" he yelled.

"Yup. Sure is. " I said with confidence.

"Stop fucking him before you and him both end up dead." He screamed. Who did this nigga think he is? He came in here like he was my man or something. He got a whole family at home and wasn't about to start one here.

"Are you done now?" I asked. With my gun still in my hand I saw he wasn't trying to leave. I pointed my gun directly towards his head.

"You know damn well you ain't about to use that." He laughed, thinking shit was funny when it wasn't.

Once I got the door open, Twan was standing there at the same time I was trying to get Donte out. When Donte looked at me, I already knew he was gone start some shit. I already knew Twan was thinking I was some hoe or something but it wasn't even like that. Wait a fucking minute, I said to myself.

"My bad ma." said Twan.

"No you stay, he was just leaving." I yelled.

"Oh, so this who you fucking?" asked Donte.

"That don't matter, you're not my man, I been asking you to leave and plus you never had the right to ask me anything." I yelled with my finger in his face.

Donte reached up and hit Twan with a two piece causing him to fall on the floor, I ran over to Twan and Donte threw me across the living room like I was a doll or something. This nigga had me fucked up in so many ways.

"Stop Donte and get out." I yelled.

"You fucking my bitch nigga? You don't know what you getting yourself into Lia I promise you don't." yelled Donte socking the fuck out of Twan. Donte was hitting him so much blood started to leak from his mouth.

"Please stop it or I'm calling the police, you're just jealous nigga." I yelled.

Donte jumped off of him, and started to walk towards me. I pulled my gun out my gown and pointed in his direction.

"You choosing this nigga over me?" He asked me with spit coming out his mouth.

"Don't come near me, I'm not your girlfriend and I don't won't you." I snapped.

Twan got up from the floor with my vase in his hand. Donte had his back turned not knowing what's going on behind him.

WHACK! WHACK!

Donte stumbled to the floor. Twan hit him upside the head with my vase. I could see the worry in Twan's eyes because he walked in on something that had nothing to do with him at all.

We finally figured out Donte wasn't dead, he was on the floor aching from the pain in his head. He got up from the floor stumbling, reaching for his gun. Blood was everywhere in my living room carpet and I was beyond pissed off.

POW!

Twan snatched my gun from my hands and shot Donte one time in his back. I didn't know if he was dead or alive, but at this moment he wasn't responding.

"My house?" I cried.

"I got you ma, you have nothing to worry about" he said.

"Where I'm gone go?" I said.

"Go to your friend house, leave right now." he said.

"What you gone do with the body?" I asked.

"I got this just leave." he demanded. I looked over at Donte one last time and seen all the blood coming from his body. I didn't know what to do or what to say, everything happened too fast for me.

I grabbed my purse and keys and called Jas telling her what was going on, I didn't worry about packing any clothes or slipping anything on. I went outside in my gown that I was wearing for Twan. I couldn't believe this shit had went down in my house.

I can't even say he didn't care about me because he did or did he? Sometimes I felt like he only wanted to keep me around so I wouldn't mess with anyone else but that wasn't gone happen. He was married to a whole freaking person. FUCK!

This nigga was really crazy over some pussy that didn't belong to him. He lost his wife and now he probably lost his life. I felt bad about how things had to happen between me and Donte but I told him plenty of times to leave and he wouldn't.

Digging in the ashtray inside my car I sparked up my blunt that I had rolled from earlier. With this stress on my back I hoped it would calm my nerves. I needed to smoke and drink my night away; I would not get over anything like this.

Hearing my phone beep, I looked down and seen I had a text from Twan.

Twan: everything's good, you have nothing to worry about. Long as your mouth stay closed they wouldn't figure out anything. Hope to see you again and I hope I didn't scare you off, I was just defending myself.

My head was full with mixed emotions. It's like part of me wanted to cry because of the death of Donte and the other part said fuck it. No, we weren't in a relationship but we've messed around for years. Yes, I loved me some Donte, but on a different level. We had that kind of low-key love, the love nobody knows about but you two.

I'm sure some females done experienced being with a married man whether you knew or didn't know he had a second family. It's not easy at all loving another chick's man. Times when you wanted to be with him at night, you couldn't because he was home being with his wife and kids. It sucks!

Jasmine

After getting the call from Lia, I was scared for my girl. I tried putting pieces together but I could barely hear anything she was saying from her screaming and yelling.

Sitting in the living room waiting on her arrival, I sent Slim a text message and asked him was he awake. Not getting a reply I put my phone down and waited for my girl to come. It kind of got to me that he didn't reply back to my message but once I noticed the time I figured he was sleep. I was not about to let insecurity ruin this relationship.

Five minutes later she was walking through the door with tears in her eyes. Her face was a mess, her body was shaking and her hair was all over her head. Not bad ass Lia. Funny right, who would have thought big bad ass Lia would ever be coming to me crying and scared?

"Donte is dead." She cried, falling into my arms.

"WHAT? WHAT HAPPENED?" I asked rubbing her tears.

"Twan asked me to come over and I told him yes, I heard a knock on my door and it was Donte. He comes in cursing and yapping off at the mouth like he was my man or something. Moments later Twan came in and that's when things hit the fan." She said rolling up a blunt. Her hands was shaking so bad I had to remove the blunt and weed from her before she lost her mind.

"Are you okay baby?" I asked.

"I don't know what's going to happen bestie; it's always some bull shit."

"Calm down baby." I replied back. I finished her blunt and gave it to her. The way she snatched it out my hand I couldn't do nothing but pray for her. Lia was a mess.

"Bestie if anything happens to me, I want you to know I love you more than anything in this world. Make sure you send me away fly as fuck." She laughed, trying to fight back her tears.

"Lia boo don't talk like that, everything will be fine. I got you baby." I said giving her a hug. I hated the way she smoked her problems away, she couldn't go a day without weed and I hated that.

***

Everything was great, especially with me and Slim. He mentioned something about me helping out with him at his youth center, which I loved. I told him I would love to, knowing I could teach those little girls a lot. This semester was over with and I wouldn't have to see GVSU for another five months.

It seemed as if these days were flying by. A month ago Lia came to my house wearing nothing but a robe and lingerie because of the incident that Twan and Donte caused at her house. She ended up getting transferred to my job with the connection of her old one. She wasn't living in Grand Rapids anymore; she was now here in Muskegon with me.

Today was the day Lia was moving into her new apartment that Twan helped her with. She tried so hard to convince me that she wasn't falling for Twan but I knew she was because of how she acted around him and talked so much about him. Even though I didn't care for him that much I still had to respect her choices. Plenty of times Twan would bring up conversations about Kenny but I always ignored them, not caring what he had to say.

I was out shopping for food to cook at her place because we were unpacking her things and we ended up getting hungry. I didn't know if I wanted to make lasagna or some tacos so I decided to grab the ingredients for both.

I was looking a mess but in other eyes I was looking good. So many guys were staring at me but I kept it to moving. I had a good man at home and there was no need to mess things up with him.

My hair was straight with a middle part and I had on my black and white Nike jogging suit with my all-black Nike Air Max's. I wasn't dressed today because it was moving day and I wanted to be comfortable.

I gathered up my groceries and was headed out the door. I got in the car and sped off in the parking lot rushing so I could get there and cook this food. Around this time of the day, I knew Slim' greedy ass would be hungry.

When I got around the corner I noticed that same white Dart kept following behind me. Making a couple false turns I was right, I was being followed.

Pulling into a parking lot, I checked my mirrors and saw the person looking in my direction. I hesitated to get out the car but I did anyways.

I was kind of scared, but I had my knife on me just in case I needed to use it today. I got out the car and waved my hand to tell them to pull up closer, to see what they had wanted. They pulled on the side of me and the driver rolled his window down and soon as I saw the face I was shocked because I couldn't believe who I was looking at.

171

My legs were shaking, my mind was racing, my eyes were watering and my body couldn't move. If looks could kill this bitch would have been dead.

I tried to run back to my car fast as I could but it was too late because he had caught up right behind me.

"Thought you would never see me again didn't you?" he said.

I couldn't even reply, I never been this scared in my life. "Do you miss me?" he asked.

"Miss you? I haven't thought about you since the day I left you at the house." I finally said.

"So you telling me you haven't thought about me not once? Was I dead or alive? Nothing? All the love making we did? I missed you." He said rubbing his hand across my face.

I knew he wanted something because why else would he come back for me after I left him for dead.

"How did you get away and how did you know where I moved?" I asked with tears in my eyes.

"Bitches like Kema you can't trust." He said with a smirk. I looked at him not understanding anything he was saying, once it finally hit me I read between the lines.

"Really? So all this time you were fucking her too? What is it that you want with me? Why did you do me the way you did? You a fucking dog ass bitch." I yelled spitting in his face.

SMACKKKK

He smacked the rest of the spit I had left out my mouth. I fell to the ground, trying to get back up but it was hard. Once I got back on my feet I ran to my truck.

"Did you guys enjoy your envelopes? We will meet again Jas." He said as he got inside his car and pulled off.

***

KNOCK! KNOCK! KNOCK

I was banging on Lia' door hoping she wasn't in the basement or nothing knowing he could just pop up anywhere.

"Damn I'm coming beating on my door like that, who it is?" she yelled.

"Lia it's me, hurry up and open the door." I screamed

"Come in baby, what the fuck happened?" she snapped.

"It was Kenney he's been following me and he said he know where I live and knows where Slim lives at, he also mentioned an envelope that I got in the mail couple months ago I never opened it up because it didn't have a name on it. Girl, all this time he was fucking Kema and she helped him find me and got him out the house." I said.

"Are you fucking serious? I knew something was up with that bitch, my vibe around her wasn't right at all, where that bitch at?" She snapped becoming a hype man. Punching the palm of her hand Lia was on ten.

"I don't think I can tell Slim about this he already crazy about me. Kenny is not gone let me off easy like this and we both know this. I'm so confused I just want to beat his ass but first I need you to ride with me to my house so I can see what's in that damn envelope he sent me." I said.

We pulled up to my house and I ran inside got the envelope and ran back outside and got in the car.

When I opened the envelope it was a small picture and once I flipped it around it was the same girl I killed in the house we lived in when I caught him cheating. What the fuck is going on? I needed answers and needed them soon. What does this have to do with Slim?

"Why would he send it to your house and then send something to Slim house, girl you gone have to tell him what's going on so he could open us his envelope and see what he got." She said.

"Girl he would kill him if he found out anything." I cried,

"Let him, y'all been together for months now, it's his job to protect you." Lia snapped.

I took her advice, we flew back to her house and soon as I got inside I called Slim' phone but I didn't get an answer. At this moment all I wanted to do was see my man and lay in his arms. Being around him, I felt I was safe from everything.

I called him three more times and he still didn't pick up the phone. At this moment, I didn't know what to think, what if Kenny had already killed him? What if he's cheating on me? Ugh, I hate feeling some type of way about stuff because it didn't do nothing but lead me into becoming insecure.

Insecurity was the last thing I wanted to invite into my relationship and that's exactly what I was doing.

"He still ain't answering?" asked Lia.

"Naw, maybe he's taking care of business." I said.

"Probably is, try calling Rock phone." she said.

"I don't have his number." I said.

"Damn me either." she said.

I sat here waiting to see if he was gone call back, I hope he wasn't out here fucking no other female while I had this bull shit going on. I looked at this picture for the longest and was admiring this young lady's beauty. She was so pretty to me. Since Kenny was alive, it had me thinking was she dead or alive as well? Ugh! I don't know what to think. I tried to remember anything I could. Coming up with small pieces but I came up with nothing.

Rock

Me and Slim been out all day fucking with the kids at the youth center. I was proud of what my nigga was doing but I really couldn't give these lil niggas any advice because the streets were in me. Only advice I could give them was to stay out the way because a bullet didn't have a name on it, and to finish school.

Chasing pros was all I knew and wanted to do, I dreamed about money so much to the point where I had to get out and fuck with it the extra-long way. Some niggas was stacking to be seen, but me I was stacking to disappear. I'm not gone lie, one day I wanted to find me a wife to enjoy all these millions with but until then I was just chillin.

"Damn, seven missed calls from her." he said.

"Shit I see you ain't the only one missing her ass." We both laughed.

"I'm gone call her back soon as I get to the crib." he said.

"You won with this one bro." I said speaking about Jasmine.

"I already know. You need to fuck with Lia crazy ass." He said, running his hands through his dreads.

"She ain't ready for this. She still is playing those kids games." I said seriously.

"I feel you bra, and it don't make since to bring her home if you still gone be dipping in the cookies with Nicole fine ass."

"Ain't she though?" I said, trying to get Nicole out my mind.

"You ready?"

"Yeah I am." He said.

Giving everybody some daps and hugs we were on our way out the door. Forgetting Slim came and picked me up, we hopped in his Range Rover and took off.

Pulling up to my crib, we made small conversation about some other shit with Lia and Jasmine. I got tired of Lia playing games with me, one minute she acted like she want me then the next she on something else. So tonight I was heading over to Nicole's to break her back out. Me and Nicole use to have a thing for each other back in the day, during the time Slim and Princess was together but once we realized we loved the streets too much we decided to just be each other's booty call.

Last week sometime I forgot to go get some condoms, so I knew I had to run to the store real fast. Wasn't no chick coming to me saying they pregnant. Hell naw, I wasn't going out like that.

"Be safe out here nigga." I said.

"You too bro." He said pulling off.

I didn't even go in the house, I hopped in my car and drove right out the drive way. Filling on my pockets I had to make sure my pistol was on me because you never know when you gone need it.

I pulled up to the gas station and seen Moe coming out the store with two other niggas.

"Aye, tell that nigga Kenny to hurry up." He yelled.

"What's good Rock?" He said walking towards me.

"Shit dawg. What you got up for tonight?" I asked him.

"Nothing, but aye check this shit out. Ace didn't tell you that they needed to re-up? He asked.

"Naw he ain't say shit like that but did you go handle that?" I said. This shit didn't sit right with me, something was definitely off. Since Ace was one of my workers he knew to call me if he needed anything. Moe was the one to drop it off to him so I don't understand why he didn't dial my number.

"You already know bro." he said dapping me up.

"Good looking." I said.

I walked into the store and purchased my condoms. Once I looked outside I noticed Moe was talking to some hoes. I don't know what the conversation was about but I seen Moe smack one of the girls across the face with a roll of money.

Moe wanted too much attention and I didn't like that. He was too flashy and that's the kind of shit that brought you too many problems.

I walked out the store and seen that nigga Kenny staring me down like he was on some gay shit or something. If I'm not mistaking this the same nigga from the other side who had problems with me and Slim years ago. We older now, so I'm probably just tripping. Shit I'm high anyways, but who gives a fuck?

Pulling off in my Charger, I didn't pay they ass no attention and proceeded to finish what I was doing. I had Peezy- Looking Crazy blasting through my speakers, thinking about all the niggas who hated me.

Before I was heading home, I made my way to my trap house to check on some shit. I pulled up and got out the car. I got to the door and walked inside with my key. Once I got inside the living room I was greeted by Mr. Jenkins.

"Everything good?" I asked him.

"Naw son. Come sit down and talk to me." He said. This was something new to me, he never had problems.

"What's up?" I asked him as we made it into the kitchen.

"I'm not feeling that friend of yours." He said.

"What friend?" I asked, letting him know he had my full attention.

"The one that do the drop offs. Every time he comes through here, he doesn't come alone. When I tell him about the shit, he tells me he knows what he doing." He sighed. "I don't trust him at all."

When he mentioned the one who did drop offs, I knew he was talking about Moe ass. As he kept going on and on my finger got trigger started to itch. I had to bite my jaw because I didn't want to cause a scene and worry Mrs. Jenkins.

"Word? Thanks for that information. I'll handle him." I said making my way to the basement.

Once I got down I walked through everything and checking it making sure it was right. I didn't have time for niggas to be down here fucking up my money.

"Ace, let me holla at you." I yelled.

"light boss man." He said smoking a blunt.

"You needed to re-up?" I asked him.

"Moe came through here earlier and handled everything." He said never taking his attention off what he was doing.

"So everything straight down here?" I asked looking around.

"Of course, I been working for you since I don't know how long. If it wasn't for you, I wouldn't be eatin. I got a baby girl at home who needs shit. I wouldn't dare fuck you over." He said. From the tone of his voice, I could tell he was serious. But I knew Ace wouldn't play me, my main concern was Moe.

"I know this shit nigga. Some shit just been going on lately, hit my line if you need me." I said waking off.

I got to the top floor and Mr. Jenkins nodded his head at me. Once I got in the car I drove off heading towards my crib. If I had to cut Moe off, it wouldn't be a problem. He was starting to fuck up and when Mr. Jenkins noticed a change I believe him.

I got home and it was now 10 on the dot. I was gone smoke me a blunt and chill out until it's time to go blow Nicole back out.

Facing this blunt, I started to think about my past. I was smart with the shit I did. I didn't carry a lot of money on me and I made sure I had more than one bank account. Slim was the second person to sign on anything of mines just in case something was to happen.

I did a lot of shit in life, fucked up shit at that. It wasn't something I was proud of and bragging about, but I can't change the past. The past could change me only if I was really ready for something new and I wasn't.

Glancing over at the time, midnight came fast as hell, I was just now putting on my shoes and shit. I wasn't into impressing nobody so all I had on was my Ralph Lauren jogging suit and some all-white Nikes. Grabbing my keys, I walked out the door.

I pulled up to her house and from the outside of it, you would think she was living rich. She had an all-white house, with a white fence around it. I knew Nicole was a hood bitch but I didn't think she was living like this. I was told a while ago, after the death of her baby daddy she took over everything he had going on.

I knocked on the door and she opened it standing in all-red lingerie with the matching heels, damnshe made a nigga second man stand strong.

"I just put my son to sleep, you can come in." she said.

Admiring her designs that flooded her house, everything in this bitch cost bands, a female that got money like a nigga was a turn on.

"You can follow me in here." she said.

"Bet."

She laid me on the bed, taking off my clothes and the last thing I had on was my boxers. She slid my dick out my boxers, and used her mouth as a tool wasting no time.

"Oh shit! Damn ma." Her mouth was putting in overtime, she swallowed my dick not leaving a part out almost having a nigga in here screaming like a lil bitch, I had to bite the inside of my jaw.

I felt my nut coming up; she kept sucking and playing with my balls letting me shoot all down her throat, swallowing it up like a pro.

"G shit." I said.

I placed her on all fours in the middle of the bed. She tooted her ass up and I rammed my dick in her.

"Right t-heer-e" she moaned out loud.

"Where? Here?" I went ever harder.

Holding her arms from the back, I was fucking her so hard I felt sorry but it still didn't calm me down.

"FUCKKKKKKK-KKK" she yelled out trying to escape.

Finally, I let her go and she climbed on top of me sliding down my dick like a stripper pole. The way she kept popping her ass on my dick had my eyes glued to the ceiling. Rotating her hips, she tightened her pussy. I can't lie, she had a nigga ready to commit.

There was no need on instructing her to do nothing, because she was already experienced.

"Fuckk." I was releasing my load and from the looks of it she was too. I felt her juices come down my dick, and I was squeezing her ass tight while she moved her hips in circles.

She showed me where her bathroom was at so I could clean myself off. And when I came back she was sitting on her bed rolling up a blunt.

"Yo man ain't coming home soon is he?" I joked.

"Don't know what those are." She replied back.

She passed me the blunt, inhaling these goods I just laid back on the bed and let my mind wonder. Shorty was a freak, as I had my eyes closed I felt the wetness from her mouth touch my dick.

She stuffed my dick and balls in her mouth, sucking and slurping up the salvia causing my toes to tap-dance. Once she tightened her jaw it was over and done with. I couldn't keep these moans in, she had me feeling like a pussy.

"You the truth." I said

"I do my best." She flirted.

"I see." I said.

"You can spend the night here if you want." She said getting out the bed.

Soon as I laid back my phone started ringing, once I reached inside my pocket it was Ace calling me.

"What's up nigga?" I said in the phone.

"Get here now." Was all he said and he hung up. I didn't have to hear nothing else.

Something was going on and I didn't know what it was. I got up, put on my clothes and headed to out the door. Once I got outside I hopped in the car and drove off. Taking my gun out the glove department I stuck it in the side of my pants.

Slim

When I got Jasmine' calls and messages, I was speeding to Lia house, carrying along a yellow envelope she told me to bring with me, for what I didn't know but I did anyway. From the sound of her voice, I could tell something was going on.

Pulling up to Lia house I jumped out the car almost forgetting to put the car in park. Running towards the door she was already coming outside to meet me.

"Baby girl what the fuck happened?" I yelled. Her right side of her face was swollen and red. Staring at her you could tell the difference.

"Listen, we really need to talk I was on my way home from class and I noticed a white Dodge Dart was following behind me I pulled up in a parking lot and I approached the car first. The driver rolled down his window and it was my ex Kenny, I never thought I would run into him, but today I did and we got in to a small argument and I pushed him out my face and that's when he hit me." She said.

"He hit you? Where the fuck is this nigga? I was pissed the fuck off, I didn't play that putting your hands on a woman especially one who belongs to me.

"It's more Slim, he knows where I live and you live, he's been following me and ain't no telling for how long, but anyways he mentioned something about an envelope he sent us. I never opened mines til after I seen him and I went and got this envelope, and when I opened it I saw a picture of a girl and on the back of it, it said YOU WOULD NEVER BE HER, you need to open yours, maybe it's a connection to something." She cried.

I untapped my envelope and took a deep breath. Once I flipped the picture over and noticed who it was I yelled "PRINCESS?" I didn't know what was going on, but I needed to find this out now. Was he the one who killed her? If so, what the fuck Jasmine have to do with it? Why did he come back for her? It's some shit going on and I was gone get to the bottom of it.

"This is your ex-girlfriend that you lost?" She asked me. She looked at me and closed her eyes. Damn, I hope this ain't her sister. I thought to myself. I never knew Princess to have any other sisters but Nicole.

"Yes this is her. Do you know her?" I asked.

"No I don't." She said looking me in the eyes.

I flipped the picture over and on the back of my picture it said Everybody ain't who they say they is. I didn't have a clue as to what he meant by that, was it something going on that I didn't know about? Shit like this made me think everybody was out to play me.

"I'm sorry, baby I really am," She kept saying sorry like it was her fault when nothing was. If he wanted problems with me then we can take it there but bringing drama to my girl wasn't gone happen.

"Baby girl no need to apologize everything gone be good." I said back to her.

"Baby, we in this together, wherever you go I'm going I know I'm nothing like Princess, I don't know anything about the streets or being a ride or die but I'm not dumb either and when my life's in danger or someone I love I know what to do, just trust me baby please." She begged.

"Jasmine, that's dead baby girl, I'm not losing another one to this shit, me and my niggas got this I just need for you to be safe and I promise I can protect myself, you know nothing about this street life I know you want to be down, but right now it's no time to teach you, it's time to get shit to cracking, you my baby man and you ain't gotta cry or worry about shit so you not doing business with me and I mean that." I said.

"She can live here, I'm sure he don't know where I'm at." said Lia.

The name Kenny sounded familiar as hell but I just couldn't put a face to it. The deeper I started to think made me get a headache because I knew that name from around here. I had to go investigate some people I use to deal with back in the day. Even though that was the last thing I wanted to do, it was needed to keep my girl safe.

***

Riding through the streets I was listening to Kevin Gates- In my feelings trying to get my thoughts together. I couldn't do nothing but think hard about the bull shit that happened. I been ducked off and I didn't want Jasmine to feel like I was angry at her so I kept my distance for some days.

Even though I knew she wanted to be there for me, it was nothing she could do because she didn't know what was going on just like I didn't.

I really didn't have time for the beefing shit, I had my life on the right track now and I didn't want to bring back the old me. I knew muthafuckas was now playing with my emotions and everybody knew when it came to Princess I didn't play.

I haven't shot a gun in years, but if I gotta put my hands on one to protect me and mines then I'm doing whatever it takes.

Why would they kill Princess is what I want to know? Why is he dragging Jasmine into this? I had a lot of shit on my mind and the only thing that could clear it all would be a fat ass blunt and some Hennessey to go with it.

I felt my phone vibrate in my pocket and once I pulled it out it was Rock calling me. He didn't know what was going on and I had to fill him in.

"Sup?" I greeted him.

"Man, that nigga Moe on some snake shit." He yelled through the phone. I knew he was pissed I could hear it all in his voice.

"Meet me at the crib nigga." I said hanging up.

Moe

A cold hearted nigga? That was me, I didn't give a fuck about nothing or nobody and there was nothing that could change my mind. A lot of niggas didn't fuck with me but I was cool with it because I was never the kind to have an army following up behind them.

This is a dog eat dog world and every nigga trying to become number one. When it came to competition, everybody was in it, people you would have never thought you would compete against. It's fucked up how money makes you see the greed in niggas, but now days everybody tryna stack, pray and stay out the way but for some of the wrong reasons.

Sitting outside the gas station I was waiting on my big brother Kenny to come out. The death of my brother which was Kenny' twin, changed him a lot and made him not give a fuck about shit either.

This was a typical Friday and didn't nobody do shit but come post up at Shell's gas station and look at the hoes walking in and out of the store, smoke some weed and drink some lean. I fucked a lot of bitches and then walked pass they ass like I didn't know em. All niggas did was sit in they cars and blast music through they speakers.

Sitting in the car I noticed something so bad and thick coming out the store. Jumping out the car I couldn't miss this opportunity so it was a need for me to get out.

"Excuse me Miss Lady." I said getting her attention.

"Hello." She said.

"What is a girl like you doing on this side of town?" I asked.

"I'm just here with some friends, but I'm ready to go home." she said pointing to a car full of girls.

"What's your name?" I asked her.

"My name is Keisha and yours?" she responded.

"My name is Moe." I said.

"Is it a way I can call you sometimes?" I asked her.

"Yes, here's my number." She said grabbing my phone.

"Aight. I'm gone call you tonight." I said walking off.

Jumping into the car I sat there waiting for Kenny to come back out. I peeped Keisha and her home girls eyeing a nigga down. I sparked up a blunt and inhaled it until Kenny came out.

I wasn't fucking with Slim and Rock no more, I been doing my own shit solo. Slim got out of prison and got to thinking that he was better than us and shit and Rock on the other hand always chased up behind him like a bitch ass nigga.

Once I left the gas station the night I ran into Rock, I told him Ace needed to re-up. It was easy for me to pull that one because I was the one Ace always called when he needed more products. Only time Rock came around is when things went bad and when he needed to do a money check.

It's a lot of shit they didn't know about me, in their eyes I was a snake but in mines I was just getting back what he took from me and mines. I called up my homeboy I was working with to let them know shit was starting to heat up, and I didn't give a fuck if Slim found out about me or not.

"Dawg?" I said onto the phone.

"What's good boy?" he asked.

"Make that shit happen." I said.

"You ain't said shit but a word." he said and hung up.

What I didn't like about Slim was that he had the kind of attitude like he couldn't be stopped and he never had security around his home or where he did business at. I wasn't wrong for nothing I did and I hope he feel my pain when I do what I do to him. I knew Slim had a lot of niggas beefing with him, but that's the thing, he was never worried about nothing, he was ready for anything that came his way.

I was getting tired and a nigga was ready to crash at the crib, but Kenny hoe ass was taking all damn day in the store. Looking at my phone I was interrupted when it started to ring.

"Wassup?" I answered.

"I been following her around all day and she keeps going into public places." he said

"Well nigga keep doing yo job, if nothing happens you won't be getting paid." I snapped.

"Yeah okay." he said.

Finally, the nigga had come out the store and behind him followed some thick bitches that looked hittable.

"Took you long enough," I said.

"You know I had to flirt with the bitches, so I can get some ass later." He said.

"Yeah whatever nigga," I laughed.

"Did Twan handle that shit yet?" he asked.

"Yeah he on it right now, I just got off the phone with him when you got in." I said.

Kenny was the only thing I had left and I couldn't dream about anything happening to him. When we lost our brother, his twin, things wasn't the same anymore.

Pulling up to my crib I shook his hand and got out the car, because this Hennessey was twenty minutes from having me off my ass and I couldn't hang with it no more. Walking inside the house, I walked straight into the bathroom to take a shower.

The water was getting cold, so that snapped me out my thoughts quick. I got out the shower I walked into my bedroom and threw on some boxers and got in the bed. A nigga was tired of coming home to an empty house; I needed a bitch or something or at least a live in booty call.

Everybody in my circle had roles to play and I prayed they didn't fuck up because I knew Slim was a ruthless nigga and didn't need an army of niggas behind him because he always handled his shit. I saw him in action millions of times. Nobody knew me and Kenny was brothers because we looked nothing alike. Jasmine didn't even know shit about me because I never came around her.

I'm originally from Detroit. I didn't share the same father as Kevin and Kenny did, we only had the same mother. My father couldn't stand my mother so he always kept me away from my brothers. Once she died Kenny tried to reach out to me, but my father didn't want me talking to them at all. I met Slim way before I met anybody else because his father and my father use to hang together back in their day. Once I came down here to visit Slim he introduced me to the long money and fast life style.

When I hooked up with Kevin and Kenny they told me they had beef with Slim because he took over the streets and made the South hungry. The day we came up with a plan to rob Slim was the day his younger sister ended up getting killed, but somebody else who had beef with him got to his spot before we had the chance. After that I left to go back to Detroit until things started to die down.

Earlier that day before Kevin got killed was the day Slim sent for me to come back and he told me what was going down. Once he mentioned he had hits on his sister death he tried calling me but I didn't answer because I couldn't take my blood out like that. The only reason Slim felt like Kevin and Kenny killed his sister was because someone on the streets got paid to make it look like us South Side niggas did it.

Jasmine

It's been two weeks since the last time I saw Slim. It's been so much going on lately and I couldn't wait to he put an end to it. I didn't know how I was gone tell him that I was the one who killed Princess. I couldn't do it, and I didn't plan on doing it. If anything, I would prefer he found out on his own time.

I couldn't believe that she was the one all this time, the girl I caught in my house fucking my man. Why would she cheat on him? Hearing him talk about how he loved her and how she was the first girl to steal his heart made me feel some type of way because I'm the reason why he felt like her death was his fault. I don't even think I'm going to see him again because being around him would make me feel guilty that I was the reason the love of his life was dead.

Out of everything that life threw at me this was one of the toughest things I ever had to deal with. It's like I wanted to tell him but then again I couldn't.

I loved that man, and can't nothing or nobody take that away. Not knowing the outcome of what's going to happen made me so terrified.

Leaving work, I pulled up to the ATM machine and reached into my purse to get my wallet out. Once I left here I was heading to my own home. I needed to get my thoughts together and think about everything that's been going on. If Kenny wanted me, he knew where I lived. I wasn't running anymore.

I got ready to take my money out the machine

WHAM!

I was hit in the mouth with a gun and I instantly felt my lip burst open. It started to burn but there was nothing I could do about it. Blood was pouring from my mouth as I received several more hits to the face. Everything around me was moving slowly, I felt dizzy as my head fell unto my steering wheel causing the horn to blow from the pressure of my forehead. I was able to move and hear everything, but I just couldn't do it at a fast pace. My vision was now blurry and the only thing I could see was the same woman who caused me to have a miscarriage.

"So we meet again?" A female said.

Once, I was able to lift my head up I put my feet on the gas, and drove out the parking lot of the bank and that's when gun shots was starting to come through my back window. I felt my tire blow off, so I knew I was out of luck.

Finally, I got out the car slowly moving towards the main street so someone could see me. I felt like I was going to pass out the more I ran. I felt my body getting weaker and weaker.

Making it to the main street I saw lights flashing and heard police sirens and that's when everything went black.

***

These lights were bright as hell, many voices were around me but I couldn't move. The more the lights shined in my face the more it was hard for me to see anything. I hated when the hospitals had these lights hanging above you head.

I felt someone hand in between mine but I didn't know who. I squeezed their hand hard trying to get their attention.

"She's up. She's up." I finally recognized Lia's voice. She yelled kissing me thousands of times on my forehead.

Once again I tried opening my eyes and when I did I spotted Slim and Lia standing over me with tears in their eyes. I tried to smile but I felt my lips painfully cracking, the feeling you get when you're shit dry and ashy on a cold day in the winter time.

"Who is this?" I muttered. I looked over to the left side of the room and found a stranger sitting by the sink. I didn't know this guy from a can of paint. Once he saw I was up and alert he jumped up and walked to the foot of my bed.

"Ma'am I know you don't know me, but I saw everything that happened to you tonight. I was parked on the other side of the street I couldn't do anything but call the police because I had my kids in the back seat and I didn't want to put there life in danger." he said. If it wasn't for this man I would be dead right now. I closed my eyes and tears fell freely. I was thankful that someone like him would do the right thing instead of leaving me for dead.

"Thank you sir we really appreciate you. If you wouldn't have done that ain't no telling what could have went down." Said Slim.

"Th-ankk you-u." I garbled. I couldn't speak clearly, but I wanted him to know I was thankful. My voice was low and dry, and not to mention my throat felt raw.

"Baby girl, I know you pissed off at me, don't be though I'm sorry for not calling you, and when I found out what had happened to you I was pissed because I wasn't there and you needed me. I'm here now and I promise to never leave again." He said. I could see the sadness in his eyes but I felt like I didn't deserve his apology because of the things I didn't share with him.

He bent down and hugged me. I did nothing but cry while trying to hug him back. I wasn't crying because he was here for me. The tears that were coming down my face were tears that had a bad meaning behind it, a meaning that would turn him to hate me.

195

"I love you sis and I'm glad you're okay." Lia finally said. She stood on the right side of me bed and wiped the tears from my face. She took some MAC lip gloss from her purse and rubbed them on my lips causing Slim to laugh.

"Love you too." I laughed.

"She could only have one person spend the night with her and someone will have to be leaving in about five minutes because visitation hours are over." The nurse said coming into the room. She walked into my room sounding like she had an attitude.

"You could stay Slim, I'll go and come up here tomorrow sometime. Get some rest sister and call me when you're up to it." Said Lia. I was kind of glad that Lia said she would leave because all I wanted to do was be with my man because nobody could make me feel safe but him.

"I love you baby girl." He whispered in my ear.

"I love you more." I said back. I felt so guilty by sitting in his face knowing I was hiding something from him.

***

Two nights later I was being released from the hospital and everything was good with me. I just had a small cut across my lip and forehead. I wished I knew who this specific chick was who kept coming after me. I didn't deal with Kenny anymore, so I don't know why she came back for me.

"Baby girl you know you coming to my crib right?" Slim stated. I knew he wanted me safe but I didn't want to crowd him in his own home.

"Why?" I asked with an attitude.

"No need to ask questions it's already done and your stuff is already moved in." He addressed. He didn't even tell me anything about this or ask me if this was something I wanted to do.

"Wow." I chuckled.

It wasn't that I didn't want to live with him but I was a big girl and could handle myself and plus I loved living on my own. I needed my space at times when I wanted to have my attitude or be in my feelings. As we were supposed to be heading home Slim was taking a different route or he caught amnesia while I was in the hospital.

"Where are we going?" I asked looking out the windows.

"Home." he said keeping it short.

Pulling into this big white house, I noticed my car was pulled into the driveway with his cars as well. The house was beautiful. He had to purchase this when I was in the hospital, I'm glad he did it because it was beautiful as hell.

"Baby this is beautiful. I love it." I said as we got out the car. Stepping inside the house I was in complete awe once I saw the inside of our new home. The living room was decorated with white and grey. We had four bedrooms and three bathrooms.

Running a nice hot bath I walked out the bathroom into his room and noticed my shoes were neatly stacked on the side I assumed was mines. He had my perfume and lotions along with my jewelry sitting neatly on the dresser.

"Ok I appreciate this but um where is the things from my apartment?" I asked looking around the house.

"I gave it away to a thrift store." He said with a straight face. I know this nigga has got to be high or something to just up and give my stuff away. I paid for everything and it wasn't cheap.

"You're kidding right?" I asked with an attitude. He looked at me and smiled.

"Check your bank account." He said walking over towards me. I picked up my phone and clicked on my bank app and seen that fifteen thousand was deposited into my account. I looked at him and rolled my eyes. Leaving out the room I walked into the bathroom and turned the water off. Removing my clothes, I sat down in the tub. This hot water felt so good against my skin.

"Why you leave out the room like that?"

"Because, I don't want you thinking I need your money. I have my own. I had things from my parents I wanted to keep." I yelled rolling the eyes God blessed me with.

"Check this shit out Jas. Being with me that independent shit goes out the window, yes I love that you independent but I do for mines. I gave that to you because appreciated you being down with a nigga. I don't ask for shit in return but to remain loyal to me. Lia was the one who got everything out your house and she told me what to keep. If you would have paid attention to the living room once you walked in you would have seen your parent's belongings." He snapped and walked out the door. Damn! I didn't mean for him to get mad, I understand he's trying to help me and all but damn.

I washed my body and got out the tub. Once I dried off, I made my way into the room and found Slim laying in the bed watching T.V.

"I'm sorry." I said.

"It's cool ma." He said back not taking his eyes off the show he was watching. I lotioned my body and joined my man in the bed.

****

Stretching and yawning this morning I woke up and didn't see Slim in the bed with me. As I made my way out the bed, I walked down the hall and saw him in the kitchen making breakfast.

"Good morning funky breath." He laughed flipping the pancakes.

"Fuck you." I said.

"Come on then." He said rubbing his dick.

"You're not ready for this." I said shaking my ass.

I went into the bathroom and brushed my teeth. As I started to walk back to Slim I heard my phone ringing. Walking in the room, I reached over the bed and picked me phone up from under the pillow.

"Who is this?" I answered the phone.

"What's up Jas baby?" Asked Kenny.

"Stop calling me that, what do you want? You did enough? I yelled in the phone.

"See bitch you always gotta get smart with a muthafucka."

Slim must have heard that I was arguing on the phone because he ran in the room and snatched the phone from my hands.

"You got one more fucking time to disrespect my lady like that, what the fuck is yo problem and what the fuck you won't with her? She ain't got shit to do with this, you got beef with me not her so leave her the fuck alone, I'm done playing yo mind games you pussy ass bitch." Snapped Slim.

"You right nigga she ain't got shit to do with this, but since she with you I'm making sure she in this now, and that's gone always be my bitch. After while she ain't gone be yours either, once she tell you what you want to know." Said Kenny and hung up. Slim looked at me and his eyes got big.

"Yo what the fuck he talking about?"

"What you mean?"

"You got something you wanna tell me?" He asked.

"No baby I don't, he just trying to upset you." I lied hoping he would fall for it.

"You sure?" He asked.

"I promise you baby."

"I bet not find out you hiding shit from me or the consequences won't be good." he said.

What the fuck was I gone do now, I wouldn't dare let this man slip away from me. We've came too far to let something fuck us up. I knew once he found out I killed Princess he was gone kill or leave me for good.

We got back to the kitchen and ate the breakfast he prepared. Eggs, pancakes, bacon, sausages and grits were on the menu.

"Thanks babe." I said drinking the last of my orange juice.

"You welcome ma, anything for you."

With all the problems going on I still wanted to get out and get some fresh air. So today I was planning on going to Slim's youth center and take the girls out shopping. Running in the room I got dressed and fixed my hair.

Wearing my all-white Burberry skinny jeans, with my Burberry Brit brown checkered shirt I had on my all-red pumps. My hair was in another middle part but instead I had those tight curls falling down my back. My full lips was coated with a nude color lipstick.

"Baby I'm gone." I yelled to Slim.

"Take my car this time and face time me until you get there." He said.

"Which car?" I asked feeling bossy. Slim had three cars and I didn't know which one I wanted to drive. He had an all-white Range Rover, A dodge Challenger and an old school Chevy.

"You choose."

I kissed his lips and made my way to the garage. I didn't know which car I wanted to drive so I picked any set of keys. Hearing the lock release on his all-white Range Rover I jumped in, arranged the seat on how I was comfortable driving.

Riding down the street I was blasting All Eyes on You by Nicki and Meek and can't forget about my husband Chris Breezy. Snapping my fingers jamming to the music I felt like I was the shit.

She was the baddest, I was the realest we was the flyest

Counting this money loving the feeling look at you now in love with a hitta

Interrupting my vibe, Slim was calling me on FaceTime. I knew he was pissed because I forgot all about what he told me to do. I already had my phone connected to his built in touch screen deck.

"Man you don't fucking listen." He said brushing his teeth.

"I'm sorry baby I really forgot." I said trying not to laugh.

"Don't do that shit again." He yelled not accepting my apology.

"I won't baby." I said.

"Where you at man?" he asked.

"Pulling into the youth center right now," I said parking the truck.

"Aight! Let me know how everything goes. FaceTime me back when you leave there." He said. He blew me a kiss and I did the same and we disconnected the call. We can be corny at times, but it's all love.

I walked to the front door and used the key to get inside, I was impressed how nice it looked. Almost wanting to cry, I was happy that he did something like this to help kids out. My baby really did his thing with this one.

"Hi, I'm Keisha." She said reaching to shake my hand.

"Hello sweetie, I'm Slim's girlfriend Jasmine." I said back.

"You're pretty." She said.

"Naw, she's a baddie." Said another girl coming into the living room.

"Thanks girl and you are?" I asked.

"Kanisha, what's your name." She asked. I could tell she was snappy and fast just by the way she approached me.

Both girls were beautiful and unique in their own way. Keisha, the one I met first had a peanut butter skin tone with long black curly hair. Her eyebrows are what stood out because they were naturally arched. With her full lips and thin eye lashes she was adorable. Kanisha reminded me so much of Dej Loaf with her short haircut. Only difference about her was her weight, she was way thicker the whole way around.

Taking a tour around the center they introduced me to a lady who seemed to be doing laundry. My eyes got big once I stared into her pretty face. Her skin was flawless and she was a light bright older woman. I couldn't get my eyes off her because she reminded me of someone I knew but I just couldn't figure it out.

"Excuse me Ma'am." I said getting her attention.

"Baby you scared the hell out of me, you must be Jasmine?" she asked giving me a hug.

"Yup that's me and your name?" I replied.

"Mrs. Latisha, honey." She said.

Mrs. Latisha and I chatted it up for a bit before I headed out with the girls from the center.

Walking towards the front door, we got out outside and jumped into his truck.

The whole ride to the nail salon they were singing and dancing to the music I was playing. It felt good to be there for someone, giving them the attention they begged for.

Pulling in the parking lot of the nail salon I grabbed my keys and we got out the car. It wasn't packed and that was a good thing.

Sitting in the nail salon about three females were laughing and gossiping like always. Flipping my hair I walked over to the sink and I felt somebody eyeballs burning a hole in my back. Once I finished I turned around and walked back to my seat.

"Isn't that the girl Kenny left for Kema?" I heard one of the females whisper to the other one. I knew they had to be talking about me because I was the only bitch present. I didn't want to set a bad example knowing I was sitting with Keisha and Kansisha

***.

The day was almost over with and the girls and I were out eating ice-cream. The day we spent at the mall I helped them pick out a million of different outfits. Slim gave me his credit card and we went bananas.

"Do you love Mr. Johnson?" asked Keisha

"Yes I do. So much," I said smiling.

"Are you in love with someone girl?" I said bumping her a little.

"No not yet. I'm just asking because I want to experience it one day." She said looking down at the table.

"Honey love is not all what people make it out to be. I mean, it can be good and it could be bad. You're still young so live your life, go to college, stack your money and then think about love. If it's meant for you to fall for someone at this age then be careful and protect your heart." I tried making it sound easy so she would understand me.

"Were you I'm love before him?" asked Kanisha

"Yes. I was deeply in love with the wrong someone. I knew I deserved more but I was afraid of someone else getting what I had. Enough about me tell me something about you girls." I said.

"My parents were murdered right in front of me when I was four years old. Every day I have dreams about the day they were killed. The guys had on black mask so I never got a chance to see any faces. Besides that I always wanted to be an author and write stories about my life and other lives. But I never had someone to share my stories with, to see the talent I was born with" Cried Kanisha.

"It's okay to cry, I'm here let it all out. I'm sorry to hear that Hun my parents were killed in a car accident so I understand your pain." I spoke rubbing her back.

Seeing the tears in these girls' eyes made me feel so concerned about their future. The thing about individuals you never know the stories behind their reasons and yet we still judge them.

"I'm nothing like what people think I am. I lived in the projects all my life. I grew up living with my grandmother and never got the chance to meet my mom. My father has been in prison for over fifteen years and I haven't got a chance to speak with him, something I would love to do but I have no connections to him at all. Basically all I had was myself. My grandmother would use my body to support her drug and money habits and that's when I gave up on everything. I always had a talent for dancing and singing but nobody ever heard my voice." Said Keisha.

"I'm so sorry you had to go through that shouldn't no one have to put their body in that kind of pain for anyone." I said. I knew this girl had a lot going on just by the way she spoke. Even though I just met them I had a strong connection with them and I really wanted to be a part of their lives.

"I would love to read your stories one day Kanisha and watch you dance Keisha. Now enough crying girls let's enjoy our day and finish our ice-cream." I said trying to cheer them up.

Making our way back to the center I decided to FaceTime Slim so we could speak with him and let him know how much fun we had. I hope he had some clothes on, knowing him he loved walking around the house naked.

"Wassup bae?" he spoke through the camera.

"Hey. I got the girls here with me." I cheerfully said.

"Hey Mr. Johnson," They said waving their hands.

"What's good ladies? Did y'all have a good time?" he asked them.

"Yes we enjoyed our day thanks to Jasmine. We put a hurting on your card too." They said making me feel good on the inside.

"I ain't tripping, that's good y'all enjoyed yourselves. Aye I'll see y'all later. Thanks baby." He said getting off the phone.

"Mr. Johnson is fine." Said Kanisha.

"Watch it girl." I said moving my index finger.

Pulling up to the center we laughed some more and got out to go inside. Once I made it inside the house was dark and nobody was here. I panicked for a minute but I didn't want to scare the girls. Reaching into my purse I pulled out my pistol and walked slowly through the hallways of the house.

"Step back girls." I whispered moving them out the way.

I heard a noise towards the basement that sounded like glass being broken so I was easing my way down the steps until I was interrupted by a scream coming from the direction of the girls.

I ran over to the girls and the only one who was standing there was Keisha so I assumed someone snatched up Kanisha. Running to the front door with my gun I noticed the same all-white Dodge Dart Kenny drove had just pulled off.

Shooting in the direction of the car I missed it by an inch. I shot at the tires not wanting to shoot inside the car because I didn't know who head I was gone hit when I knew Kanisha was inside.

"WHAT THE FUCK DOES HE WANT WITH ME?" I yelled running through the house.

Pulling out my phone I sent Slim an emergency text letting him know to get here fast. Searching through the house for the others I couldn't find anyone.

"Stay right here and don't move Keisha. Do you understand me?" I demanded. I left her upstairs inside the closet. I also texted Slim and let him know where she was hiding at because I didn't want her to come out when she heard them coming in, knowing any movement he would of shot.

As I got closer to the basement I saw Mr. Smith lying on the ground with his head split open and there was Mrs. Latisha on the side of him. Wrapping my hair in a messy bun I pulled the sleeves of my shirt up and lifted Mrs. Latisha up on the couch. Checking her body I noticed blood was coming from between her legs. RAPE, was the only thing that came to mind.

As I opened her legs to observe the inside of her I could tell she had been brutally raped. Her body was shivering nonstop. I searched around the basement seeing if I could find any towels to clean all the blood up from her. Once I found towels I turned the light on and she winced in pain from the bright lights shining in her eyes. Both eyes were black and her nose was covered in blood.

"Can you hear me? Are you okay?" I yelled. Seeing her like this did nothing but make me weak for her. I never thought Kenny would take this to a whole different level. Trying to fight the tears back I couldn't hold them in anymore. I took covers from the laundry room and placed them over Mr. Smith's dead body. The sight of him made me sick inside feeling like everything's that's happening is because of me.

"They to-oook him." She stumbled over her words.

"Took who?" I asked puzzled for a minute trying to figure out who she was talking about.

"Ant." She softly said.

"Did you see any faces?" I asked.

"No just two guys and one girl." she said

Just as I got ready to carry her up the stairs Slim and Rock was running down the stairs not okay with what he was seeing Slim started punching holes in the wall.

"They got Kanisha and Ant and Mrs. Latisha was raped badly we have to call the police and get her to the hospital." I cried.

"What happened?" He calmly asked. One thing about Slim he never let anyone see him sweat about shit. He could have the biggest attitude and you wouldn't know it. He looked over at Mr. Smith and began to lose his mind.

I told him what happened from the time I walked inside the door and gave him the information Mrs. Latisha provided me with. All he could do was hold his head into his lap and pray that God watches over the kids.

***

Sitting in the hospital with Mrs. Latisha and Keisha I was glad everything was okay with her. She lost a lot of blood and had patches over her eyes but that was all. The nurses wanted to keep her overnight to monitor her. Visiting hours were over and Slim was out tearing the streets up looking for Kenny, Kanisha and Ant. Bad as I wanted to help Slim out he wasn't going for it at all.

"I'll be back to see you tomorrow afternoon." I said kissing her on the cheek. She shook her head and squeezed my hand letting me know she would be okay. Walking out her room we got on the elevator and I said a silent prayer for the return of Kanisha and Ant. As we jumped into my car I looked over at Keisha and noticed she was still freighted.

"Everything's gone be okay baby. I hate that you had to see all of that." I said rubbing her shoulders. We drove off the parking lot heading to my home. Keisha asked me if she could spend the night at my house and I told her of course.

Pulling inside the driveway I checked the app on my phone lurking inside my home making sure I didn't see any movement from anyone because I knew Slim wasn't home. Not seeing anyone we got out the car and I still had my gun glued to my side.

As we got inside the house I took my shoes off and plopped down on the couch staring into space. I had so much on my mind that I needed to get off and the only people I could tell everything to was Slim and Lia but Princess was the only thing that stopped me from talking to Slim because I couldn't tell him what I wanted to. I felt like the world was now crashing down on me and there was no way around it. It's not easy to just walk away from someone you're in love with and I know that for a fact.

Times like this I wish my father was here because he was the only one who seemed to take away my problems and stress, well at least it felt like he did, I guess that's that fatherly love.

"Keisha? Who do you live with hun?"

"My female cousin. She's my legal guardian until I turn 18 in a couple of months." She said not taking her eyes off her phone.

"Somebody's in love." I teased her trying to ease my mind away from the problems I was having.

"It's nothing like that he's just a friend." She said smiling. I called Slim's phone and didn't getting nothing but the voicemail. I began to worry about what was going on. I got up and went to the bathroom to run me some bath water.

Once my bath water was finished I snatched off my clothes and eased inside the tub letting the hot water soothe me. At this point nothing felt better than sitting in a tub full of hot water; it seems as if the steam took away my problems.

"Baby girl." I heard Slim say as I jumped up. I was so comfortable that I fell asleep in the bath tub not knowing Slim was even home.

"How long was I sleep?" Noticing the wrinkles around the tip of my fingers answered my question. There wasn't even anymore more bubbles and the water was very warm.

He washed my body and helped me out the tub carrying me into the room. Things like this is are what makes my love for him stronger. He was so affectionate and warmhearted. A thug with a good heart described my man in so many ways. At this point in my life I knew there wasn't any other place I would rather been, then with him.

"Any luck?" I asked. Studying his facial expression, I knew he hadn't found them and it was starting to stress him. He laid me down in the bed and wrapped his hands around me not saying a word.

"Why aren't you talking to me Slim?" I asked removing his arm from around me. I sat up in the bed and stared into his glossy brown eyes, waiting for an answer.

"I love you, just go to sleep ma." Was all he said, I couldn't sleep knowing that those kids were out suffering because of my mess. They had nothing to do with that and that's what was killing me the most. "Lord bring those babies back safe." I said before I closed my eyes.

Slim

Me and Rock spent all kind of nights dropping bodies to only bring back nothing. Wasn't anybody mouths open like usual. This time when you needed a rat, they were nowhere to be found. Kenny had to be paying cash money to keep his end quiet.

All I wanted to do was live my life the right way but it's always those ones who hate to see you doing something good. I can't lie this shit had me fucked up in the head. I found myself smoking and drinking more than I usually do just to ease my mind.

It's a lot of niggas who hated me because of the things I did in my past. I don't regret shit I did, its life and being in the streets I already knew how the game went. I never walked around saying I was a big bad wolf but I wasn't for games either. I did shit, and didn't learn from it because I found myself doing the same mistake over again. Ain't shit out here easy and living damn sure wasn't.

As far as Mr. Smith death, I was hurt and upset that he had to lose his life because of my foolishness. Knowing he had no family I got his body cremated and it sat on the table inside my living room.

Mrs. Latisha was doing fine, recovering very well and I thanked God about that every day because I couldn't be accountable for another life. As of now, the youth center was closed down because it wouldn't be the same with all the tragedies that happened. With Mrs. Latisha being without a job I gave her 20k. I even talked Keisha into moving in with her.

Beneath everything that's been going on today I was surprising Jasmine with a mini-vacation to Miami. Rock knew to call me if he heard anything about Kanisha and Ant. He was my right hand man and he made my problems his whether he had anything to do with it or not and that's why I never questioned his loyalty.

"Baby get up," I said smacking her on the ass.

"It's still early Slim." She whined stretching across the bed. Even with her morning breathe and scratchy voice she was still perfect to me.

Finally getting her out the bed we got up and handled our hygiene's. She didn't know where I was taking her so I told her we were going to see my parents and she went along with it, she was excited but I knew once she found out we were going to Miami she would be even more..

"I'm nervous as hell right now baby I hope your parents will like me." She said fixing up her hair.

"Girl my momma gone love you I know she will and my dad might try to holler." We both laughed. I knew my parents would love her on some real shit.

"You ready?" I asked her.

"Sure is. Let's go." She said. I grabbed her bags and mine and we headed out the door. Soon as we made it outside Rock and Lia were pulling up. They were taking us to the Airport just in case some niggas felt like coming to my crib they will see our cars parked outside. As we finished loading up the car we walked across the street to Mrs. Latisha house to make sure she was good before we headed off.

"How you doing lady?" I asked ask she opened the door to let us in.

"I'm fine, you kids don't have to check on me gone out and have some fun because you out of everybody deserves It." she said waving her hand. We hugged her and went on our way.

Pulling up to the Airport, Rock helped me unload all of our belongings and Lia and Jasmine was hugging each other as if we were moving away for good.

"Nigga stay on it. Hit my line if anything." I said dapping up Rock.

"Slim I ain't new to this shit, I'm true to this. Just enjoy yourself with your lady in Miami nigga." he shot back causing me to laugh. I knew he had everything under control but I didn't want him feeling like he had to handle it all by himself if some more shit went down.

The look Jasmine had on her face was priceless. Seeing her smile made me happy. This wasn't the way I planned for her to find out thanks to Rock, but he knew nothing about it being a surprise so I couldn't even be mad that he spilled the beans, as my grandma would say back in the day.

"Nigga, why you lie?" She said mushing me in the arm. I picked her up and swung her around in excitement, long as my lady was happy I was too and there was nothing nobody could do to fuck up this vacation, well I hoped.

***

I forgot all about Jasmine telling me she was scared to fly until she damn near snatched my arm off.

"Ma, yo grown ass gone be good." I laughed.

"I know but I'm still nervous and shut up." She said hitting me in the shoulder.

"Man I hate that fucking scar on your lip." I said. Since she was robbed at the ATM machine she had a permanent mark slit across her lip that would never disappear and every time I saw it, it pissed me off.

"Is it ugly?"

"Naw baby you're still beautiful I just hate the fact I wasn't there to protect you because none of that shit would have happened." I said.

"It's fine just promise me you'll never leave me again." She said.

"I promise." I kissed her.

Seconds later Jasmine had fallen asleep and I was up listening to Future.

Hours later we were getting off the plane. We ended up renting a Chevy Malibu. The ride on the plane made my body stiffen up and all I wanted to do was relax once we got inside the hotel but of course my spoiled brat thought otherwise and there was no way I could tell her no.

Driving in Miami Florida was different than what I was used to. I been a lot of places but never been here and I loved the sight I was seeing. Jasmine had her phone out taking pictures of everything she saw. Once we pulled up to Four Seasons Hotel Jasmine was in awe. The sight was beautiful.

***

"Come give me a kiss ma."

"Oh I got something you could kiss." she said walking towards me.

"Oh? Do you?" I said and smacked her on the ass.

"Slimmm stop were in public." She said licking her lips.

"So, this mine and I could do what the hell I want with it." I said with an attitude.

Instead of us going out for dinner she decided to have lunch here at the Miami Edge Steak & Bar. The restaurant was nice and the guests were real friendly. I had so much stress built up inside me I couldn't wait to get back to the room and beat her back in taking my frustrations out on her pussy.

Enjoying our food we talked about different things and shared some good laughs.

"Baby I'm ready to go back up now. We can do more tomorrow." She said wiping her eyes.

"Okay cool." I said hoping she wasn't getting tired because I needed some pussy.

Satisfied with the room everything looked nice. I sat down kicked my shoes off and laid back while Jasmine rolled me up a blunt. A lady who could roll was a blessing in my eyes.

"So what are we doing after our shower?" she asked.

"I don't know whatever you want." I said taking the blunt she had just finished. I inhaled this bomb ass weed letting it take me to another level.

"Let's fuck in the shower and finish the rest in the bed if you don't tap out." Looking back at her she was so serious and just hearing that come out her mouth already had my johns pleading for attention.

"Lead the way." I insisted.

Letting the water run directly on the both of us. I admired her body, every time I looked at her I feel like it's my first time seeing it. Lifting up her left leg on the head of the shower, I started sucking on her thighs and blowing on her clit just to tease her.

"Stop playing." She moaned.

The movement from her body was letting me know she wanted more. Opening up her lips with my tongue, I sucked on her clit then nibbled on it like a mouse. Latching on to it I began pleasing her. I felt like my tongue was in competition with the hot water dripping down her clit. I heard many women say they used the shower to slightly please them, when they man wasn't there to do it.

Gliding my tongue from the front to the back, I played with her nipples with the tip of my fingers and stuck my tongue in the inside of her ass sucking up the mess I made like a vacuum cleaner.

"Shittttt." she moaned.

I took the tip of my thumb and massaged her clit and started to suck on her left breast. A couple minutes after she was having an orgasm and that shit always turned me on.

"You stand up it's my turn." she said.

She got on her knees and took a mouthful of my dick into her mouth rotating her head in circles playing with my balls at the same time. She tickled the tip of my dick with the tip of her tongue.

"Oh shit" I groaned out sounding like a lil bitch but baby skills was something serious.

"Let me hit that from the back ma" I said slapping my dick across her ass. Standing inside the shower against the glass sliding door she put her hands on one side of the tub and her legs on the other side.

Ramming my dick in her from the back, gripping one of her ass cheeks with my hand I used the other one to pull her hair.

"Go faster baby." she moaned.

What made her say that? I made her toot her ass up and I went to work, no slow type, I pounded her shit.

"Shit, Slim I'm finna cum-mm" she moaned. I always made sure she got hers first and I got mine second.

She was squirting all on my dick, causing my dick to throb. I knew I was coming next and it felt so good. I picked her up and she bounced up and down clapping her ass on my dick with her hands on the shower wall.

"Damn girl." I said releasing my load inside her.

"Slim, why didn't you pull out? We didn't use a condom." she said.

"Ok and you gone be my baby mama." I said.

"Baby mama? Oh NO! You got me all the way fucked up nigga." She snapped.

"Calm down baby." I laughed.

After we finished showering we made our way to the room and jumped into the bad wearing nothing but our birthday suits.

I loved the kind of relationship we had I never made her do anything she didn't want to. She understood my past and I understood hers. At first it was kind of hard being together knowing we come from different families but our bond is unbreakable and the first time I laid eyes on her I felt the connection.

"What's wrong boo?" I asked.

"Nothing, just thinking." she said.

"Something is up talk to me." I said rising up in the bed. I sat her between my legs and started to massage my fingers through her hair.

"I just am thinking will we ever have the same relationship you and Princess had? Hearing how you were in love with her always has me in my feelings because she was actually down for you."

"Man don't be thinking about that I'm here because I want to be, I love our relationship and I love you, no matter what happen you gone always be my baby. And what you mean down?" I said.

"I meant like yo gangsta bitch she did everything you did." she said.

"Y'all two different people, just because you were nothing like her don't mean shit I love you for you. You're smart, intelligent and got goals. Baby girl you can't base our relationship on the one I had with her. Trying to be like her is what's gone kill our relationship because I'm with you for you." I said.

"It's one more thing that's been bothering me for years." she said.

"What's that?" I asked.

"I don't think I could have any kids due to the miscarriage I had. I don't want you to suffer from not having kids because I can't." she cried.

"Baby girl don't cry I might be a thug but I believe in God and I know anything is possible." I said.

After that talk she ended up falling asleep and I kissed her on her cheeks. If I didn't show it or say it enough I really appreciated Jasmine sticking by a nigga side.

Lia

Pulling up to my house I sent Twan a text message asking him if he could come over. Tonight I just wanted to cuddle and be in the arms of someone. With some much on my mind I wanted to be home with someone I knew who cared. Something was up with me and I wasn't feeling it one bit. I think I allowed myself to fall in love with this man. It felt good for the moment but the change in me wasn't a good feeling.

Me: are you busy?

Twan: naw ma, I'm chillin what's up?

Me: come through tonight I need you

Twan: ok cool give me about an hour or two

Me: bring a bottle; pay you when you get here

Twan: I got you ma, you don't owe me anything.

Getting out the car Rock grabbed me by my arms pulling me back in. I almost forgot who he was, cause he was about to get cursed out.

"Man why you be playing?" asked Rock.

"How am I playing? You got so many chicks running around. I don't need the drama." I responded with an attitude.

"Chicks? Girl, I'm a single man. I don't have anybody. I wouldn't be on you so hard if I did." He said seriously.

"Look Lia I been feeling you for a minute, I'm not with the childish games. We grown right? I know you want me just as bad as I want you." He said.

"You got some much confidence, I like that. How are you so sure?" I asked.

"Look how you act around me; you wouldn't be in this car having this conversation with me right now. Drop that square ass nigga and get with a real one like me," He said.

"Give me a call sometimes Rock." I said putting my number in his phone.

"You got it ma." He said pulling out the drive way like a happy kid or some shit.

Walking to the front door I looked over my shoulders, checking my surroundings. Approaching the front door I got a funny feeling in the bottom on my stomach. Standing inside the living room something didn't feel right so I grabbed my mace off the dining room table. Every time I got a gut feeling that something wasn't right 9 times out of 10 I ended up being right.

At this moment all I wanted to do was talk to Jasmine but she didn't answer her phone and neither did Slim. As the tears filled my eyes I tried holding them in because I didn't want to stress something that was just a feeling.

I poured me a glass of wine and started to listen to my Ciara CD and soon as And I came on I jumped right in my feelings; see shit like this was new to me. I turned the music down because I could have sworn I heard some glass break from my kitchen.

Grabbing my knife I slowly walked towards the kitchen. One thing my Nana taught me was to start swinging in every direction I could. Getting closer I heard my floor squeaking so I knew right then somebody was in my house and something was going to happen.

I couldn't see anything because my kitchen light was turned off, so I wouldn't know if anything was coming towards me or not, all I know is I started swinging as I heard the footsteps approaching me. I was swinging the knife and spraying mace everywhere like the crazy bitch I was. I quickly said a prayer asking God to forgive me for everything. Who would want to kill me? I asked myself thousands of times.

WHACK! WHACK! Two blows to my stomach, that caused me to fall to the floor in pain.

"Oucchhh…..what do you want?" I cried. Holding on to my stomach I knew I wasn't gone make it out here alive, my knife had landed on the other side of the kitchen floor.

"Bitch, get the fuck up, and shut the fuck up" he said.

I was trying to get back up but I couldn't because they began kicking me in the stomach and pistol whipping me across my face. The weaker I got I knew there was nothing I could do, everything was dark and I lost control.

"Didn't I tell you on the phone that you didn't know what you were getting yourself into? You should have stopped then but instead you wanted to continue being captain save a hoe." One of the guys said.

"I didn't get a chance to fuck you after the club the exact day I met you, but now I got the chance and I hope your pussy good as Donte said it was." He stood over me and pulled down my pants and used spit to rub across his dick.

"Damn you already wet bitch." He said as he rammed his dick inside me. As bad as I wanted to scream out in pain the feeling I was receiving wasn't letting me. It felt so good but I had to remind myself this wasn't no romance it was forced sex.

"Enough mutha fucka." The first guy yelled. I already knew I was going to die. All I could do is hold my face and shed millions of tears on the wood that covered my floor. Never thinking that anything like this could happen to me, I didn't understand why my death had to be so painful. Was this my punishment for sleeping with Donte? My body was shaking from all the hits that were coming my way. I lived a good ass life, all the pain, joy, dick, hurt, laughs, and tears it was something that I'll never forget.

I didn't even care anymore I was in so much pain. At this moment dying was all I wanted to do instead of being tortured.

"You either gone tell me where I could find Jasmine or you'll take the bullet that was meant for her." He said as I heard the sound of the gun clicking.

"Do what you got to do dumb mutha fucka" I said. I knew if Jasmine was in the situation she'll do the same for me, we had that kind of love. I enjoyed every memory I had with her and she'll forever be in my heart. My sister, best friend and of course my ride or die bitch.

POW! POW!

Jasmine

This was the best vacation I had ever taken and Slim made sure of that. He always spoiled me and of course I didn't think I deserved it but he did. Today we were on our way shopping and later on we were catching a movie.

Pulling up to the Aventura Mall the smile on my face was huge. I've heard so much about this mall but I never got the chance to see it for myself and today I did. With all the money I had saved up I was planning on cashing out in every store.

The first store we walked in was Burberry and I went to grabbing everything I liked, not having to check the price tags. At this moment I was acting like those children who weren't use to nothing and even though I was use to shit like this I just never had the chance to visit the stores since I always ordered online.

"This trip for you ma, here you go I want you to enjoy yourself." Slim said handing me his credit card. I didn't want to seem so desperate but I took it anyway and I was planning on grabbing him things with my money.

I had to grab Lia ass something too because if she was here with her man I knew she would do the same so it was only right if I brought her some gifts back. As I handled my purchase in Burberry we were on our way to the next store. Stepping inside the Louis Vuitton store I fell in love with all the purses I saw.

"Let's go to the True Religion store." He said as I paid for my new purses. Once we got there Slim grabbed us both at least three pairs of pants each and a couple of shirts. As we shopped around in other stores I got tired so instead of us catching a movie I wanted to relax and drink inside our room. I didn't like leaving the hotel for nothing, it was beautiful and comfortable.

As we pulled in front of the hotel we handed our keys over to the valet guy and we walked inside heading to our room. I couldn't wait to get home and show Lia her gifts. Speaking of her I wanted to give her a call once we got situated to see how she been.

Making it to the room I dropped the bags and jumped on the bed. Slim came over and took off my shoes and said he was going to run me a bath. Things like this mattered so much to me, I swear it did.

***

Soaking my body in the tub Slim was facing me. I didn't think we could actually fit inside the tub together but I was wrong.

"Baby girl I really appreciate you staying loyal and being down for me. A lot of girls like you can't handle a dude like me, and you proved me wrong. Some girls would have been left after going through a situation like this. This street shit ain't easy or fun. Plenty of nights I would wake up in sweats knowing I was the cause of the family screaming and crying. I only did the shit to make sure me and my family had no worries and once I got my money straight I promised myself I would never do it again. First time I laid eyes on you I knew you were mine. I told myself I would never fall in love with anyone else after I lost Princess, but I fooled myself." He said. I could see the pain in his eyes and after all the tears just fell down his face knowing I was the one to blame for Princess Death. Should I tell him now or wait?

"That's deep Slim I never heard anything from nobody like this I don't know how the game goes but like I told you before I'm not leaving your side and I'm rolling with you til the wheels fall off whether anybody likes it or not. I don't know how your life was back in the day, but from what you telling me I know it was rough, baby everybody wasn't born with a silver spoon so I understand you had to do what you had to do to survive. I love you baby no matter what happens you're a good person and you have a good heart and never let anyone tell you different." I said whipping his tears away.

"You know I love you more." He said leaning in to kiss me. "Now are you with the shits or nah?" He asked pointing down to his 10 inch dick. I looked at him and told him for sure. We washed ourselves and he carried me out the bathroom into the room.

"Which lotion tonight?" he asked.

"Whatever one you want to smell." I flirted.

He walked over to my suit case and got out my Viva la Juicy body set. Un-wrapping my towel he started to rub my body down with the lotion. It felt so good and all I wanted to do was roll on top of him.

"Tonight you sleeping naked." he said looking at my body.

"Well I'm getting all the covers cause you not gone have me cold." I laughed.

"We got body heat." he joked.

I got up from the bed making my ass jiggle just to tease him and checked my phone to see if Lia had called me but she didn't and now I was starting to get worried because I didn't have a text or anything. As I called her phone twice I got the voicemail and that wasn't like her.

"You got him up and ready."

"I'm worried about Lia she haven't called or texted me." I wined ignoring the statement he made about his dick.

"She okay baby, her and Rock probably fucking." He laughed.

"Them two? Ain't no telling because I saw it coming." I said.

"Come over here and forget about them." He insisted. He laid me across the bed kissing and sucking all on my neck. Picking me up he wrapped my legs around his neck where my juice box was facing his mouth, shoving his tongue inside he feasted on it like it was Thanksgiving. At this moment anything that was on my mind a while ago had now disappeared.

"Mmmmmm" I moaned as he vibrated his tongue across my clit. Slim was between my legs eating like he hasn't ate anything in days. His tongue tap danced around my juice box in all kind of ways.

"Baby, slow down. Shi-tttt." I moaned pushing his head back. He reached up and grabbed my nipples. My eyes was rolling nonstop, throwing my head back I wrapped my legs tighter around his neck.

"Get on top" he demanded me.

Riding was my hobby, so I knew exactly how he liked it. He slammed me down on his dick and I started riding him from the back. Holding on to his ankles I bounced up in down like I was jumping on a trampoline.

He lifted one of my legs up, placing me in a splits position getting nothing but dick deep inside me. I popped and twerked my ass on his dick like I was in a dance competition.

"Fuck it up then." He said smacking my ass.

"Ba-baby I'm cum-min" I moaned. He flipped me over placing me on all fours making sure I was ass up and face down. He shoved his dick inside me hard as fuck, causing me to hit my head on the headboard. I placed my hands in front of me twerking my ass back and forth.

"Ohhh shittt." I moaned.

I arched my back causing him to go deeper and started to clap my ass.

"Fuck-kk Ma." He said as he released his seeds in me once again. I was huffing and puffing like I just ran laps around the White House. I just fucked the shit out my man, but I can't front so I'll just say we fucked the shit out of each other.

Slim

I woke up to my phone ringing back to back. When I finally got up I noticed it was Rock blowing up my line. Something bad had to happen because he never called me like that unless it was an emergency and that's what I hoped it wasn't. I got up from the bed and went outside to the balcony and dialed his number back. Jasmine was still sleeping and I didn't want to wake her.

"Damnnigga this better be important." I snapped.

"The streets talking nigga, I been hearing around Kenny got niggas out on yo head and he paying 10 bands to have you brought to him, and yeah he got them kids bro." he said.

"On my head huh? Everybody knows Slim ain't for any games. Once we get back we on all bull shit and that's on my mama. I need Kanisha and Ant back in good shape. I don't need an army of niggas out looking for Kenny, I want to find him myself and kill him by my damn SELF." I yelled through the phone.

"You got it nigga. Let's get this shit to crackin like the old days. They must not know what we capable of but their damn sure finna find out. When you touching back down?" He asked through the phone.

"Tomorrow morning." I said.

"WHAT THE FUCK?" he yelled.

"What nigga? What's going on?" I asked.

"Lia picture just ran across the news saying she was murdered last night." He screamed.

"You sure it's her? Fuck that go to the airport now." I yelled.

"Say no more." He said hanging up the phone.

229

FUCK! I didn't know how to wake Jas up telling her that her best friend was murdered last night, knowing she was just saying she missed her. Hearing that news just fucked my head up. Besides me Lia is all she got and I know for sure she wasn't gone take this easy. DAMNDAMN DAMN!

"Baby girl, get up we gotta go" I yelled.

"What's wrong Slim what we leaving for?" she said looking confused.

"Baby, I'm sorry to say this, but Lia was murdered Rock just called me and told me." I said looking at her. Her eyes got big and she began to break down. I knew she was hurt, hell I was hurt too.

"OMG, I can't believe this shit, why? I can't keep losing people I love, people close to me. Slim baby why?" she cried. All I could do was hold her while she cried on my chest, she just couldn't accept the fact her one and only best friend was gone so she kept calling Lia phone trying not to believe it.

I packed our stuff up fast, and the quicker we got ready the faster we would hit the road. Rock should already be at the airport but we just needed to make it. Hearing Jas cry made me sick to the stomach. Each time something happened to someone it was because of me. I hated the way pussies came after the other person loved ones instead of facing you, the one they got beef with.

***

Silence was going on the whole ride home. I was happy we caught a plane back that was getting ready to leave. All Jasmine did was cry and I hated to see a woman cry especially the one I love when I knew I couldn't stop her tears.

"Baby everything gone be okay trust me and my word I got you, and Kenny gone get what's coming to him." I said wiping the tears that fell from her eyes. I couldn't lose focus; I had to be strong for her and myself. She needed me the most and I was gone be there every step of the way doing whatever she requested.

"I just don't understand. Slim I think Twan have something to do with this. He's Kenny best friend and I know what he's capable of. I just don't understand you have to believe me." she cried.

Pulling up to the house Rock helped me unload his car with everything and plus more.

"Hit me up when you can nigga." Said Rock.

"Bet." I said.

Walking up to the house I checked the mailbox and saw another envelope with no name on it.

"I hope it's a connection to Lia's death." She said.

Once we made it inside the house we walked into the living room and plopped down on the couch. Opening up the envelope it was more pictures. Once I flipped them over I couldn't believe what the fuck I was staring at.

WHACK! WHACK!

"So you weren't gone say shit to me?" I yelled as I backhanded Jasmine causing her to fly across the living room floor.

"Yes, I promise you I was." She cried.

"When Jasmine?" She held her head down and tears poured down more. I felt bad due to the fact she had just lost her best friend but I was hurt also, to find out she was the one who killed Princess.

"This shit isn't a fucking game, many times I told you about her and how I felt and this is the kind of shit you did?" I snapped punching a hole in the wall.

"Is it true?" I asked.

"Yes, let me explain first please." She cried. "Remember I told you I found Kenny in the house fucking a female? It was her, PRINCESS. The day we got the pictures is the day I was gone leave you alone. I didn't know how to tell you or what to say." She sobbed. "I promise you Slim I never wanted to hurt you, I didn't tell you because I loved you and didn't want to leave you."

I couldn't even respond, there was nothing left for me to say. I didn't believe in putting my hands on a female but it all happened out of anger.

"I'll leave. I'm sorry." She said as she grabbed the bags that was already packed not touching anything she bought from the mall.

I was lost for words; I didn't even run after her. After all I did for her, showing her how it felt to be treated like a woman and not just some bitch she played me like I was just that soft ass nigga she was used to. I shared with her things from my past that I never told anybody else. At this moment I didn't trust anybody. Was Rock playing me too?

"I don't know what's going on Slim but I know that girl loves you." Mrs. Latisha said barging into my man cave. She must have come in once Jasmine went out because I don't remember seeing her.

"Why hold something in so important?" I asked hitting the blunt.

"Maybe she cared about your feelings and couldn't find the exact words to say to you." She said.

"You right, but I can't deal with her at this moment, I'll end up doing something I regret." I said honestly. I pulled another blunt from my ashtray and sparked it up. What she was saying might have been true, but I couldn't stand to look in Jasmines face any longer. It was gone take me a long time to get over this.

"That's my daughter Slim. I know it and I could feel it." She said with her head down.

"Who?" I asked removing the blunt from my mouth.

Moe

Getting rid of Lia wasn't a hard job especially with the help of Twan, our plan worked better, having him get Lia to fall for him we got as much information we needed. It's fucked up how love works. My next plan was to kill Jasmine or Slim or both at the same damn time and not shed a fucking tear. I had enough money to leave town, I just wanted to kill this nigga and dip but Kenny insisted that I stay and get pay back for Kevin.

Working with Slim I paid attention to his every move and then waited for the right timing to do what I had to before it be done to me. I envied him, he was made of money, smelled like money, looked like money and every word that came out his mouth was MONEY. The greed in me wanted everything. I wanted to have enough money that would last the rest of the days God gave me on this earth. Once I got rid of everything and everybody I was moving overseas somewhere, starting over.

Tonight I had a date with Keisha and I was picking her up from her place. Once she texted me the address I made my way over to her crib. Once I pulled up I called her and told her I was outside waiting for her arrival. Looking at the doors I noticed she was coming out wearing a short black dress with some sandals and had her hair braided in that 3-D jumbo braid hairstyle. She was bad as fuck and that made we want her more than I did before.

"What's up Ma?" I spoke to her.

"Hey what's going on?" she responded.

Pulling off in the parking lot we were headed out to eat. We've been talking for a minute now and not once did she offer her goods and that made me want her more. I always ran to the bitches who gave it up the first night I met them, but Keisha was way different than that. I'm slowly started to fall for lil mama but I'm not sure if she feel the same way. With all the shit going on around me I needed a bitch to disappear with once I got this money and if she played her cards right she could be the lucky winner. I never was the nigga to fall in love all I did was fuck bitches and kept it to moving.

"Why you so quiet? I asked her breaking the silence that was going on.

"I don't know I'm not a talker." She said.

"But it's different when we texting." I laughed causing her to smile. As we pulled up to Red Lobster I helped her out the car and we made our way inside. We walked passed a group of friends and they eyes were glued to us so she grabbed my hand and pulled me closer to her like I was her nigga. I didn't trip, I let her do her but the shit was funny to me.

"So tell me about you." I said trying to get to know her a little more.

"What is it that you want to know?" she asked back.

"Anything you want to tell." I said.

"Well I'm currently living with my aunt I don't have any brothers or sisters and I love to dance and sing. I'm 18 and I plan on going back to school next semester." She said.

"Is that right? You gone dance for me?" I flirted.

"Maybe," She winked her eye. I was enjoying the conversation but the way her breast was sitting up in her dress always made me drool out the corner of my mouth.

"Tell me about you now." She said making sure I had her attention.

"I'm not from here, I was raised mostly by my father and I'm the youngest of my two brothers on my mom side and I love getting money." I said.

"Where do you work?" She asked. The question threw me off a little but I had no choice but to keep it real, I couldn't start off as a liar.

"Look at me ma. What you think?" I sighed as I threw my hands up giving her a chance to figure it out.

"Mhm." She responded dryly.

We finished up our food and had small talk. I didn't know if shorty was digging to head to the room with me but I hope she didn't deny my offer.

"You ready ma?" I asked.

"Don't call me that I'm not your mother." She was so feisty but it did nothing but made my dick hard.

"My bad shorty." I said grabbing her hand.

"You wanna stay the night with me?" I asked her hoping her response would be yes.

"Sure I don't mind." I helped her get inside the car and we drove off.

"Why you so nervous?" I asked her.

"Who said I was nervous?" She laughed.

Once we pulled up to the hotel room she looked at me and her mouth dropped.

"Um is this where we staying?" she asked pointing to the hotel.

"Yes, you got a problem with it?" I asked her.

"Hell yes. I'm not a hoe, what did you think? I thought we were going to your house or something." She yelled rolling her neck.

"Chill ma, I know you're not a hoe. I won't do anything you don't want me to do. Just chill with me here tonight." I tried calming her down. I did want to fuck her but I wasn't gone pressure her into something she didn't want to do.

"You better be lucky I like you." She winked getting out the car.

"Is that right?" I said licking my lips.

Once we settled in I ordered some movies and helped her get comfortable. As I laid back I scooted her closer to me and she laid down on my chest. Future Trap Niggas started blasting from my phone interrupting our chill-time. I got up and walked towards the table to grab my phone, whoever wanted my attention wanted it bad because the caller didn't hang up.

"Speak to me." I answered the phone.

"You won't believe this shit nigga." Kenny spoke through the phone.

"Spit it out bitch." I yelled.

"The lil bitch you fucking with know Jasmine and Slim to well." He barked to me. "I think she setting you up."

"You lying nigga? You got evidence." I said. For the moment I felt like she was setting me up on some snake shit but I had to keep it cool until Kenny hit me with the information I needed to catch this bitch in a lie.

"Check your phone in about two minutes, I got pictures coming through." He said then hung up. I sat down in the chair across from the bed waiting for those pictures to come. She was asleep on the bed and all I could do is stare at her as I felt my blood

237

rising. Soon as I laid my head down on the table my phone beeped letting me know I had a notification.

This shit was too good to be true because there it was Jasmine, Keisha and Kanisha walking into the nail salon together and the other picture was her sitting outside his youth center.

"What are you doing?" she screamed.

Slim

I was missing the hell out of Jasmine but there was no way I could be around her. I understood why she couldn't come to me but to hide something like that was very dishonest and I couldn't respect it at all. Jumping out the bed I walked inside the bathroom to handle myself. This was the day I was gone put shit into action. I was dressed in my all black sweat suit and a pair of black timberland boots. A few of my niggas found out where his trap house was located and we took it upon ourselves to invade his privacy. I got my old crew back and I wanted to give these bitch ass niggas what they were asking for.

Walking into my closet, I grabbed my favorite guns and made my way out the door. Once I got outside Rock was already there waiting on me.

Lia's funeral was tomorrow morning and I knew Jas needed me. Even though it's a lot of shit going on I'll still be a man and be there by her side.

"Bro what time the funeral start tomorrow?" Asked Rock

"I think 11 fam you coming?" I said.

"You know I am I can show my respect for shorty." He said.

"A real nigga," I said.

Riding down the street we met up with everybody and discussed what was going on. People lives were on the line and there was nothing I wanted to do to fuck things up.

"Is there anything else we need to discuss? Does everybody understand their role? If shit gets fucked up you will not be getting paid." I yelled loud and clear.

"We understand boss man." Said one of my homies.

"Yea boss man is back." I said putting my guns on me.

Creeping down the street I noticed three cars were parked outside of Kenny's warehouse. I didn't know how many he had inside and I really didn't give a fuck.

Making my way towards the back, I could see inside the tiny window behind the building. The first person I noticed was Ant and he was tied up in a chair with his back against me but Kanisha was nowhere to be found.

Kicking the back door in we couldn't hear or see anything. The only thing that was noisy was water hitting the floors. Once I walked inside, I stopped at a door which looked like an office door. When I looked through the window I couldn't do nothing but put my head down.

The image I seen wasn't right at all something I didn't want to see. Ole dude had Kanisha kneeled down sucking his dick, but I knew she was being forced to do it.

"Kanisha? What the fuck you doing?" I yelled.

"Who the fuck is you?" asked the young dude fumbling for his gun.

"Let her go now." I demanded, pointing the gun to his head.

"Do you my nigga." He said yanking a hand full of her hair.

POW! POW!

I pumped some lead into his head twice and watched his worthless body fall to the ground. Kanisha ran over to me with tears and embarrassment in her eyes.

"It's okay, stay behind me." I told her.

Soon as we got into another hall we heard gunshots coming towards our way and we fired back not caring where they were heading. With Kanisha on my heels and screaming I had to get her out of here fast and not slow.

We made it inside the room Ant was in and noticed he was surrounded by three guys with masks on. One had their guns pointed on us and the other had his gun pointed towards Ant.

"Who sent you here?" asked the middle man.

"I sent myself I run shit myself." I yelled standing like the certified boss I was.

"Let him go I'm telling you this is something you don't want." I said raising my gun up higher.

"You sure about that?" he asked.

POW!

"NOOO! WHAT THE FUCK?" I yelled.

Seeing the way Ant hit the ground made me sick to my stomach. That's it, I couldn't take no more of this shit. I released lead in every body that was standing in front of me with my guys on my heels following behind me. It's been a while since these hands been on a gun but today broke the record. I done woke the fuck up.

"That's enough man the niggas dead." Said Rock. We picked up Ant body and headed out the doors.

"Ant can you hear me?" I yelled holding him in my arms. He wasn't responding but I could see his lips move.

"Ant don't do this to us we need you man; your like my brother I never had." Cried Kanisha. As we made it outside, everybody went their separate way except for me and Rock.

We pulled up to the nearest hospital and took him inside. As they laid his body on the stretcher I couldn't do nothing but shake my head. I needed him to make it, he needed to pull through. He was a strong lil nigga and I knew he would fight this.

I needed to smoke to clear my mind. Every day it was something going on and I couldn't escape my problems for nothing because they kept surrounding me.

"Family of Antony Wilson?" the nurse spoke. We got up and walked over to them getting ready for the news they had for us.

"With the grace of God he made it, but it will be a while for him to recover. The bullets hit his lungs. I know you guys want to see him now but he has to rest." I looked up and thanked God for answering my prayers.

***

Pulling up to my house something didn't feel right when I approached it. If this was my last chance at life I wanted to call Jasmine and my parents to let them know that I loved them.

"You good bro?" Asked Rock.

"Yeah nigga, I'm cool." I lied.

Getting out the car I walked towards my crib and I could smell some food cooking from somewhere but I knew it wasn't coming from my house. I reached in my pocket and grabbed my gun holding it on the side of me just so I can be prepared for the drama.

Walking in the house my nose instantly started jumping from the smell of good food cooking inside my kitchen.

"What's for dinner?" I asked looking in the eyes of my baby girl.

"Slim you scared the shit out of me." she said. She was wearing some boy shorts and a spaghetti strap t-shirt. Her hair was freshly done, and she looked beautiful as always.

"I'm sorry boo." I said.

"We're having Garlic Bread, Shrimp Alfredo and Salad." she said.

"It's almost ready?" I asked rubbing my growling stomach.

"Put that gun down." She said.

"Kanisha go shower Jasmine gone get you some clothes." I said.

"Where's Ant?" she asked me with tears in her eyes. I let her know that everything was okay with him and she agreed on going to speak with his family with me.

  I went into the bathroom and washed my hands and got myself together. I was glad she was back home, but where the fuck did she stay at?

"Aye Jas?" I yelled running in the kitchen.

"Come eat." She said.

Kanisha was still in the shower and tomorrow I was taking her to the apartment with Mrs. Latisha and Keisha. I made a mental note to ask Jasmine if she would take her to the doctors to make sure everything was okay because ain't no telling what those bitch ass niggas did to her.

She had the table set up and food on three plates. After she prayed I planned on asking her millions of questions.

"Is Kanisha joining us?" she asked

"Probably not this soon, She got a lot going in right now." I said.

"Slim, I'm sorry for not telling you. I didn't know how to come to you and tell you because I loved you and hearing you talk about her so much and realizing how much you loved her I felt like I shouldn't tell you about her cheating." She said.

"It's cool baby whatever happened ain't nothing we could do about it I mean I was pissed off but I still wanted you and there wasn't nothing to chance that. I love you man and you bet not leave this house no more and we gone get through this shit." I said.

"Do you know why she would cheat on you Slim?" she asked.

"To be honest I really don't."

"Did you miss me?" she asked.

"Hell yeah baby I couldn't stop thinking about you." I said honestly. Jasmine had my heart now and wasn't nothing or nobody coming between that. At some point in my life, Princess had it but once I found out she was cheating, I instantly lost the love I once had for her.

"Aye? Where the hell did you stay at?" I asked changing the subject.

"At my guy friend house." She said.

"What the fuck you mean yo guy friend?" I said clenching my jaw.

"I'm playing baby." She laughed.

"Aye, don't fucking play with me girl." I said.

"You're crazy." She said.

"So where did you stay?" I asked.

"Hotel." She said.

After dinner we took us a shower and were now chillin. I kicked my feet on the table and rolled me up a blunt while I scanned through the channels to find me something on T.V. She came in the living room and joined me on the couch, sitting on my lap and I could look and tell that something was on her mind. I put the T.V on mute, and started rubbing her pretty lil feet.

"What's on your mind?" I asked.

"Tomorrow, I don't think I can do it." She said.

"You gotta be strong baby girl I know dealing with things like that ain't easy but you and I both know Lia wouldn't want you crying." I said.

"I know but Slim this shit don't seem real to me I keep having dreams that she alive and somebody got her hiding." She said.

"Word? Those are just dreams baby girl." I said.

"Yeah I know but the shit seems so real." She said.

"Promise me something." I said.

"What's that?" she turned around to face me. She looked at me with those light brown eyes and I placed my hand on her head, running my fingers through her hair.

"If anything happens to me you won't be down here stressing." I said.

"Baby I can't promise you that and you know it." She said.

"I don't want you to be down here crying and stressing shit baby, its life something that's gone happen. Whether its death, jail or prison for me. I chose this lifestyle and I have to live it to the fullest." I said.

"Don't talk like that Slim." She said laying her head on my chest.

"I love you." I said, pressing my lips to hers.

"I love you more." She said accepting my invitation.

"I'm finished Mr. Johnson. I just want to sleep." Said Kanisha walking into the living room. I knew Kansisha was ashamed to look at me.

"Jasmine go handle her." I said as I closed my eyes to let my thoughts override me. I never pictured my life to be like this when I was released from prison.

"Baby. Why didn't you tell me?" Jasmine asked coming back into the living room.

"Everything gone be ok now, I promise you that." I said.

"She can't stop crying Slim." She said.

"I understand that, I feel so bad." I said.

"Just hold me please." She said lying across my chest.

"And I'm never letting you go." I whispered in her ear. I picked her up and laid her back on the glass table that sat in between our furniture. Looking at her in her eyes she was so fucking beautiful to me.

"You one of a kind ma." I said.

"Is that a bad or good thing?" she asked.

"Let me show you." I said.

Moving her thong to the side, my lips met with her lips in the middle of her legs and she tasted so sweet. I used my tongue as her personal cleanser, licking and sucking the life out her. There was nothing I wanted with any other female when I had all of this at home.

"Gawddddd." She yelled throwing her head back.

Right before I knew it, her juices flooded my face and I sucked every bit of it up, still licking not giving her time to catch her breath.

"I guess it's a good thing." She said blushing.

***

Dressed in my white Armani Suit, Jasmine was matching my fly wearing her all-white Armani women pants suit. Walking out the doors, it was time for Lia's funeral and Jasmine was holding up pretty good but I know when we got there she was gone break down again but all I wanted her to know was that I'll never leave her side again.

"Baby you good?" I asked.

"Yea I'll make it." She said.

On our way pulling up to the church I saw how many cars it was and Jasmine noticed Kenny's car and pointed it out.

"This nigga so fucking disrespectful how the hell you have the nerves to come sit up in somebody funeral knowing you're the reason they're dead." She yelled.

We walked inside the doors together and all eyes were on us. A lot of people showed Lia some love by coming out to show their respect. I had a feeling something was going to happen but I knew it was the wrong place to handle things at but I stayed ready no matter what.

A couple of Lia's friends and family members got up to say some special memories about her. Jasmine knew she was going to break down but she got up and said something anyway.

She walked up to the front of church with tears rolling down her face, and the first person she laid her eyes on I figured was Kenny because of the look she held for the longest. Once my eyes followed hers I had to double look because I couldn't believe who I was staring at.

Jasmine

I couldn't believe I just buried my best friend, my sister the only person I had in my life. The only person I knew who wouldn't have turned their back on me. I knew I wouldn't be able to handle looking at her lying inside that casket so I got a closed one. Me and Lia did a lot of things together and the memories was something I couldn't and wouldn't get over.

She may have been a feisty chick, but she was a good person with a magnanimous heart. She was so sweet and pure. How can I live without her? How can I sleep without her? We were like night and day. Who was I going to run to when I had problems with my relationship?

"How did you sleep?" asked Slim

"I didn't sleep." I said.

"Baby I wanna share something with you." He said sitting me up on his lap.

"What's that? I can't take anymore heartaches Slim." I said staring into those gloomy eyes.

"Mrs. Latisha believes Lia is her daughter." He said.

"What? How does she know that?"

"The night we got into it was the night she said it."

"I'm not sure about that Lia grandmother told us she was dead." I said shaking my head.

We were under the impression for years that Lia's mother and father was dead. Jumping out of bed, we walked into the bathroom and handled our morning hygiene. Today was the day I was finally going to meet Slims parents. After Lia's funeral we went and sawAnt and he was doing damn good. We met his parents and even though they seemed not to care we still chose to be there for them.

"Baby you got everything?" he asked.

"Yes I do let's go because I'm ready." she said.

Wearing a pair of my Miss Me jeans with my white blouse and white pumps I was ready to enjoy the time from home. I knew Slim had a lot under his belt and I didn't want to frustrate him more than what I was already doing. I was glad he didn't choose to leave me for good. I knew I wanted to live the rest of my life with Slim. All I wanted to figure out was why Princess did him the way she did.

When everything boils down I didn't want to live here anymore, I wanted to get out of Michigan and find peace somewhere else. Too many losses I took and there were no more reasons to be here.

We pulled up to a beautiful family home. It wasn't too small or too big since it was just his mother and father. I hesitated to get out the car for a minute but Slim basically snatched me out like I was being kidnapped.

***

Sitting at the dinner table my stomach was doing the naenae inside. His mom had Collard greens, macaroni and cheese, fried chicken, dressing and for dessert there was peach cobbler. The tension between him and his father was thick; the whole time we sat here they said no words to each other.

"So what is it that you do sweetie?" His mom asked me.

"Well I'm attending school at GVSU and I work at Mercy Hospital as an assistant."

"Good girl. I'm glad my son finally found him a woman with some sense." She said winking her eye at me.

We shared a couple laughs and ate well. I helped his mom clean up the kitchen and we danced around like she was my biological mom. Things like this made me weep for my parents every day. As we finished cleaning it was time for me and Slim to head back to the room.

"I enjoyed dinner and I hope to see you again." I said kissing her cheek.

"I enjoyed your company hun now don't you be a stranger and please keep my son out of trouble." Slim hugged his mom and we were on our way.

Pulling up to the hotel I stood outside while he parked his car. I texted both girls to check on them and to see what they were up to. Not receiving a text from Keisha bothered me a little. Lately, we haven't seen her or heard from her. As I tried reaching out to her she ignored me and my calls. Mrs. Latisha even said herself that Keisha's been missing in action so we all figured she went back to her aunt's house. Once we made it to our room we settled in and I was so full I didn't want to do nothing but lie down and take a nap.

Hearing a knock on the door made us both jump up. Rock, Slim's parents, Kanisha and them was the only ones who knew we were out of town. Slim got up and walked to the door but he didn't see anybody but as he turned around the knocking continued.

"Mr. Johnson it's me."

"Keisha?" I asked hoping off the bed.

"Something ain't right baby back up." He whispered to me. I didn't know how the hell Keisha got all the way down here to

Flint and I damn sure wanted to find out. Grabbing my gun out my purse I stood by my man side.

Seconds later the door was being kicked down and Slim pushed me into the bathroom. When I got up off the floor, I stood to my feet and as I peeked around the corner I couldn't believe the body that was behind the gun which was pointed at Slim's head.

"Everybody ain't to be trusted." Said the gun holder.

POW! POW! POW!

TO BE CONTINUED………..

CPSIA information can be obtained at www.ICGtesting.com
Printed in the USA
LVOW06s0430151215

466611LV00001B/209/P

9 781518 797187